O. Henry

The Gift of the Magi

And Other Stories

✺ by ✺

O. Henry

ILLUSTRATED BY MICHAEL DOOLING

Afterword by Peter Glassman

BOOKS OF WONDER
WILLIAM MORROW AND COMPANY
New York

Published by William Morrow and Company, Inc.
1350 Avenue of the Americas, New York, NY 10019 and
Books of Wonder
16 West Eighteenth Street, New York, NY 10011

Printed in Hong Kong.

3 4 5 6 7 8 9 10

Library of Congress Cataloging-in-Publication Data
Henry, O., 1862–1910.
The gift of the Magi and other stories/by O. Henry;
illustrated by Michael Dooling; afterword by Peter Glassman.
p. cm.—(Books of wonder)
Summary: An illustrated collection of fourteen short stories reflecting various
aspects of American life at the turn of the nineteenth century.
ISBN 0-688-14581-7
1. Short stories, American. [1. United States—Social life and customs—
1865–1918—Fiction. 2. Short stories.] I. Dooling, Michael, ill. II. Title.
III. Series. PZ7.H3964Gk 1997 [Fic]—dc20 96-30639 CIP AC

Books of Wonder is a registered trademark of Ozma, Inc.

For the man in the doorway
with the pale, square-jawed face,
keen eyes, and a little white scar
near his right eyebrow.
—M.D.

CONTENTS

ILLUSTRATIONS

A
RETRIEVED
REFORMATION

guard came to the prison shoe shop, where Jimmy Valentine was assiduously stitching uppers, and escorted him to the front office. There the warden handed Jimmy his pardon, which had been signed that morning by the governor. Jimmy took it in a tired kind of way. He had served nearly ten months of a four-year sentence. He had expected to stay only about three months, at the longest. When a man with as many friends on the outside as Jimmy Valentine had is received in the "stir" it is hardly worthwhile to cut his hair.

"Now, Valentine," said the warden, "you'll go out in the

morning. Brace up, and make a man of yourself. You're not a bad fellow at heart. Stop cracking safes, and live straight."

"Me?" said Jimmy, in surprise. "Why, I never cracked a safe in my life."

"Oh, no," laughed the warden. "Of course not. Let's see, now. How was it you happened to get sent up on that Springfield job? Was it because you wouldn't prove an alibi for fear of compromising somebody in extremely high-toned society? Or was it simply a case of a mean old jury that had it in for you? It's always one or the other with you innocent victims."

"Me?" said Jimmy, still blankly virtuous. "Why, warden, I never was in Springfield in my life!"

"Take him back, Cronin," smiled the warden, "and fix him up with outgoing clothes. Unlock him at seven in the morning, and let him come to the bull pen. Better think over my advice, Valentine."

At a quarter past seven on the nex t morning Jimmy stood in the warden's outer office. He had on a suit of the villainously fitting ready-made clothes and a pair of stiff, squeaky shoes that the state furnishes to its discharged compulsory guests.

The clerk handed him a railroad ticket and the five-dollar bill with which the law expected him to rehabilitate himself into good citizenship and prosperity. The warden gave him a cigar, and shook hands. Valentine, 9762, was chronicled on the books "Pardoned by Governor," and Mr. James Valentine walked out into the sunshine.

Disregarding the song of the birds, the waving green trees, and the smell of the flowers, Jimmy headed straight for a restaurant. There he tasted the first sweet joys of liberty in the shape of a broiled chicken and a bottle of white wine—followed by a cigar a grade better than the one the warden had given him. From there he proceeded leisurely to the depot. He tossed a quarter into the hat of a blind man sitting by the door, and boarded his train. Three hours set him down in a little town near the state line. He went to the café of one Mike Dolan and shook hands with Mike, who was alone behind the bar.

"Sorry we couldn't make it sooner, Jimmy, me boy," said Mike. "But we had that protest from Springfield to buck against, and the governor nearly balked. Feeling all right?"

"Fine," said Jimmy. "Got my key?"

He got his key and went upstairs, unlocking the door of a room at the rear. Everything was just as he had left it. There on the floor was still Ben Price's collar button that had been torn from that eminent detective's shirt band when they had overpowered Jimmy to arrest him.

Pulling out from the wall a folding bed, Jimmy slid back a panel in the wall and dragged out a dust-covered suitcase. He opened this and gazed fondly at the finest set of burglar's tools in the East. It was a complete set, made of specially tempered steel, the latest designs in drills, punches, braces and bits, jemmies, clamps, and augers, with two or three novelties invented by Jimmy himself, in which he took pride. Over nine hundred dollars they had cost him to have made at ——, a place where they make such things for the profession.

In half an hour Jimmy went downstairs and through the café. He was now dressed in tasteful and well-fitting clothes, and carried his dusted and cleaned suitcase in his hand.

"Got anything on?" asked Mike Dolan, genially.

"Me?" said Jimmy, in a puzzled tone. "I don't understand. I'm representing the New York Amalgamated Short Snap Biscuit Cracker and Frazzled Wheat Company."

This statement delighted Mike to such an extent that Jimmy had to take a seltzer-and-milk on the spot. He never touched "hard" drinks.

A week after the release of Valentine, 9762, there was a neat job of safe-burglary done in Richmond, Indiana, with no clue to the author. A scant eight hundred dollars was all that was secured. Two weeks after that a patented, improved burglar-proof safe in Logansport was opened like a cheese to the tune of fifteen hundred dollars, currency; securities and silver untouched. That began to interest the rogue-catchers. Then an old-fashioned bank safe in Jefferson City became active and threw out of its crater an eruption of banknotes, amounting to five thousand dollars. The losses were now high enough to bring the matter up into Ben Price's class of work. By comparing notes, a remarkable similarity in the methods of the burglaries was noticed. Ben Price investigated the scenes of the robberies, and was heard to remark:

He gazed fondly at the finest set of burglar's tools in the East.

"That's Dandy Jim Valentine's autograph. He's resumed business. Look at that combination knob—jerked out as easy as pulling up a radish in wet weather. He's got the only clamps that can do it. And look how clean those tumblers were punched out! Jimmy never has to drill but one hole. Yes, I guess I want Mr. Valentine. He'll do his bit next time without any short-time or clemency foolishness."

Ben Price knew Jimmy's habits. He had learned them while working up the Springfield case. Long jumps, quick getaways, no confederates, and a taste for good society—these ways had helped Mr. Valentine to become noted as a successful dodger of retribution. It was given out that Ben Price had taken up the trail of the elusive cracksman, and other people with burglar-proof safes felt more at ease.

One afternoon Jimmy Valentine and his suitcase climbed out of the mail hack in Elmore, a little town five miles off the railroad down in the blackjack country of Arkansas. Jimmy, looking like an athletic young senior just home from college, went down the board sidewalk toward the hotel.

A young lady crossed the street, passed him at the corner and entered a door over which was the sign "The Elmore Bank." Jimmy Valentine looked into her eyes, forgot what he was, and became another man. She lowered her eyes and colored slightly. Young men of Jimmy's style and looks were scarce in Elmore.

Jimmy collared a boy that was loafing on the steps of the

bank as if he were one of the stockholders, and began to ask him questions about the town, feeding him dimes at intervals. By and by the young lady came out, looking royally unconscious of the young man with the suitcase, and went her way.

"Isn't that young lady Miss Polly Simpson?" asked Jimmy, with specious guile.

"Naw," said the boy. "She's Annabel Adams. Her pa owns this bank. What'd you come to Elmore for? Is that a gold watch chain? I'm going to get a bulldog. Got any more dimes?"

Jimmy went to the Planter Hotel, registered as Ralph D. Spencer, and engaged a room. He leaned on the desk and declared his platform to the clerk. He said he had come to Elmore to look for a location to go into business. How was the shoe business, now, in the town? He had thought of the shoe business. Was there an opening?

The clerk was impressed by the clothes and manner of Jimmy. He, himself, was something of a pattern of fashion to the thinly gilded youth of Elmore, but he now perceived his shortcomings. While trying to figure out Jimmy's manner of tying his four-in-hand he cordially gave information.

Yes, there ought to be a good opening in the shoe line. There wasn't an exclusive shoe store in the place. The dry-goods and general stores handled them. Business in all lines was fairly good. Hoped Mr. Spencer would decide to locate in Elmore. He would find it a pleasant town to live in, and the people very sociable.

Mr. Spencer thought he would stop over in the town a few days and look over the situation. No, the clerk needn't call the boy. He would carry up his suitcase himself; it was rather heavy.

Mr. Ralph Spencer, the phoenix that arose from Jimmy Valentine's ashes—ashes left by the flame of a sudden and alternative attack of love—remained in Elmore, and prospered. He opened a shoe store and secured a good run of trade.

Socially he was also a success, and made many friends. And he accomplished the wish of his heart. He met Miss Annabel Adams, and became more and more captivated by her charms.

At the end of a year the situation of Mr. Ralph Spencer was this: he had won the respect of the community, his shoe store was flourishing, and he and Annabel were engaged to be married in two weeks. Mr. Adams, the typical plodding country banker, approved of Spencer. Annabel's pride in him almost equaled her affection. He was as much at home in the family of Mr. Adams and that of Annabel's married sister as if he were already a member.

One day Jimmy sat down in his room and wrote this letter, which he mailed to the safe address of one of his old friends in St. Louis:

Dear Old Pal:
    I want you to be at Sullivan's place, in Little Rock, next Wednesday night at nine o'clock. I want you to wind up some

little matters for me. And, also, I want to make you a present of my kit of tools. I know you'll be glad to get them—you couldn't duplicate the lot for a thousand dollars. Say, Billy, I've quit the old business—a year ago. I've got a nice store. I'm making an honest living, and I'm going to marry the finest girl on earth two weeks from now. It's the only life, Billy—the straight one. I wouldn't touch a dollar of another man's money now for a million. After I get married I'm going to sell out and go West, where there won't be so much danger of having old scores brought up against me. I tell you, Billy, she's an angel. She believes in me; and I wouldn't do another crooked thing for the whole world. Be sure to be at Sully's, for I must see you. I'll bring along the tools with me.

Your old friend,
Jimmy

On the Monday night after Jimmy wrote this letter, Ben Price jogged unobtrusively into Elmore in a livery buggy. He lounged about town in his quiet way until he found out what he wanted to know. From the drugstore across the street from Spencer's shoe store he got a good look at Ralph D. Spencer.

"Going to marry the banker's daughter are you, Jimmy?" said Ben to himself, softly. "Well, I don't know!"

The next morning Jimmy took breakfast at the Adamses'. He was going to Little Rock that day to order his wedding suit and buy something nice for Annabel. That would be the first time he had left town since he came to Elmore. It had been more than a year now since those last professional "jobs," and he thought he could safely venture out.

After breakfast quite a family party went downtown together—Mr. Adams, Annabel, Jimmy, and Annabel's married sister with her two little girls, aged five and nine. They came by the hotel where Jimmy still boarded, and he ran up to his room and brought along his suitcase. Then they went on to the bank. There stood Jimmy's horse and buggy and Dolph Gibson, who was going to drive him over to the railroad station.

All went inside the high carved oak railings into the banking room—Jimmy included, for Mr. Adams's future son-in-law was welcome anywhere. The clerks were pleased to be greeted by the good-looking, agreeable young man who was going to marry Miss Annabel. Jimmy set his suitcase down. Annabel, whose heart was bubbling with happiness and lively youth, put on Jimmy's hat and picked up the suitcase. "Wouldn't I make a nice drummer?" said Annabel. "My, Ralph, how heavy it is. Feels like it was full of gold bricks."

"Lot of nickel-plated shoehorns in there," said Jimmy, coolly, "that I'm going to return. Thought I'd save express charges by taking them up. I'm getting awfully economical."

The Elmore Bank had just put in a new safe and vault. Mr. Adams was very proud of it, and insisted on an inspection by everyone. The vault was a small one, but it had a new patented door. It fastened with three solid steel bolts thrown simultaneously with a single handle, and had a time lock. Mr. Adams beamingly explained its workings to Mr. Spencer, who showed a courteous but not too intelligent interest. The two children,

May and Agatha, were delighted by the shining metal and funny clock and knobs.

While they were thus engaged Ben Price sauntered in and leaned on his elbow, looking casually inside between the railings. He told the teller that he didn't want anything; he was just waiting for a man he knew.

Suddenly there was a scream or two from the women, and a commotion. Unperceived by the elders, May, the nine-year-old girl, in a spirit of play, had shut Agatha in the vault. She had then shot the bolts and turned the knob of the combination as she had seen Mr. Adams do.

The old banker sprang to the handle and tugged at it for a moment. "The door can't be opened," he groaned. "The clock hasn't been wound nor the combination set."

Agatha's mother screamed again, hysterically.

"Hush!" said Mr. Adams, raising his trembling hand. "All be quiet for a moment. Agatha!" he called as loudly as he could. "Listen to me." During the following silence they could just hear the faint sound of the child wildly shrieking in the dark vault in a panic of terror.

"My precious darling!" wailed the mother. "She will die of fright! Open the door! Oh, break it open! Can't you men do something?"

"There isn't a man nearer than Little Rock who can open that door," said Mr. Adams, in a shaky voice. "My God! Spencer, what shall we do? That child—she can't stand it long in there. There isn't enough air, and, besides, she'll go into convulsions from fright."

Agatha's mother, frantic now, beat the door of the vault with her hands. Somebody wildly suggested dynamite. Annabel turned to Jimmy, her large eyes full of anguish, but not yet despairing. To a woman nothing seems quite impossible to the powers of the man she worships.

"Can't you do something, Ralph—try, won't you?"

He looked at her with a queer soft smile on his lips and in his keen eyes.

"Annabel," he said, "give me that rose you are wearing, will you?"

Hardly believing that she heard him aright, she unpinned the bud from the bosom of her dress, and placed it in his hand. Jimmy stuffed it into his vest pocket, threw off his coat, and pulled up his shirtsleeves. With that act Ralph D. Spencer passed away and Jimmy Valentine took his place.

"Get away from the door, all of you," he commanded, shortly.

He set his suitcase on the table, and opened it out flat. From that time on he seemed to be unconscious of the presence of anyone else. He laid out the shining queer implements swiftly and orderly, whistling softly to himself as he always did when at work. In a deep silence and immovable, the others watched him as if under a spell.

In a minute Jimmy's pet drill was biting smoothly into the

steel door. In ten minutes—breaking his own burglarious record—he threw back the bolts and opened the door.

Agatha, almost collapsed, but safe, was gathered into her mother's arms. Jimmy Valentine put on his coat, and walked outside the railings toward the front door. As he went he thought he heard a faraway voice that he once knew call "Ralph!" But he never hesitated.

At the door a big man stood somewhat in his way.

"Hello, Ben!" said Jimmy, still with his strange smile. "Got around at last, have you? Well, let's go. I don't know that it makes much difference, now."

And then Ben Price acted rather strangely.

"Guess you're mistaken, Mr. Spencer," he said. "Don't believe I recognize you. Your buggy's waiting for you, ain't it?"

And Ben Price turned and strolled down the street.

THE
ENCHANTED
PROFILE

T here are few caliphesses. Women are Scheherazades by
birth, predilection, instinct, and arrangement of the
vocal cords. The thousand and one stories are being told
every day by hundreds of thousands of viziers' daughters to
their respective sultans. But the bowstring will get some of 'em
yet if they don't watch out.

I heard a story, though, of one Lady Caliph. It isn't pre-
cisely an Arabian Nights story, because it brings in Cinderella,
who flourished her dishrag in another epoch and country. So,
if you don't mind the mixed dates (which seem to give it an
Eastern flavor, after all), we'll get along.

15

In New York there is an old, old hotel. You have seen woodcuts of it in the magazines. It was built—let's see—at a time when there was nothing above Fourteenth Street except the old Indian trail to Boston and Hammerstein's office. Soon the old hostelry will be torn down. And, as the stout walls are riven apart and the bricks go roaring down the chutes, crowds of citizens will gather at the nearest corners and weep over the destruction of a dear old landmark. Civic pride is strong in New Bagdad; and the wettest weeper and the loudest howler against the iconoclasts will be the man (originally from Terre Haute) whose fond memories of the old hotel are limited to his having been kicked out from its free-lunch counter in 1873.

At the hotel always stopped Mrs. Maggie Brown. Mrs. Brown was a bony woman of sixty, dressed in the rustiest black, and carrying a handbag made, apparently, from the hide of the original animal that Adam decided to call an alligator. She always occupied a small parlor and bedroom at the top of the hotel at a rental of two dollars per day. And always, while she was there, each day came hurrying to see her many men, sharp-faced, anxious-looking, with only seconds to spare. For Maggie Brown was said to be the third richest woman in the world; and these solicitous gentlemen were only the city's wealthiest brokers and businessmen seeking trifling loans of half a dozen millions or so from the dingy old lady with the prehistoric handbag.

"You have a face exactly like a dear friend of mine—the best friend I ever had."

The stenographer and typewriter of the Acropolis Hotel (there! I've let the name of it out!) was Miss Ida Bates. She was a holdover from the Greek classics. There wasn't a flaw in her looks. Some old-timer in paying his regards to a lady said: "To have loved her was a liberal education." Well, even to have looked over the black hair and neat white shirtwaist of Miss Bates was equal to a full course in any correspondence school in the country. She sometimes did a little typewriting for me, and, as she refused to take the money in advance, she came to look upon me as something of a friend and protégé. She had unfailing kindliness and good nature; and not even a white-lead drummer or a fur importer had ever dared to cross the deadline of good behavior in her presence. The entire force of the Acropolis, from the owner, who lived in Vienna, down to the head porter, who had been bedridden for sixteen years, would have sprung to her defense in a moment.

One day I walked past Miss Bate's little sanctum Remingtorium, and saw in her place a black-haired unit—unmistakably a person—pounding with each of her forefingers upon the keys. Musing on the mutability of temporal affairs, I passed on. The next day I went on a two weeks' vacation. Returning, I strolled through the lobby of the Acropolis, and saw, with a little warm glow of auld lang syne, Miss Bates, as Grecian and kind and flawless as ever, just putting the cover on her machine. The hour for closing had come; but she asked me in to sit for a few minutes in the dictation chair. Miss Bates explained her absence and return to the Acropolis Hotel in words identical with or similar to these following:

"Well, Man, how are the stories coming?"

"Pretty regularly," said I. "About equal to their going."

"I'm sorry," said she. "Good typewriting is the main thing in a story. You've missed me, haven't you?"

"No one," said I, "whom I have ever known knows as well as you do how to space properly belt buckles, semicolons, hotel guests, and hairpins. But you've been away too. I saw a package of peppermint pepsin in your place the other day."

"I was going to tell you about it," said Miss Bates, "if you hadn't interrupted me.

"Of course, you know about Maggie Brown, who stops here. Well, she's worth forty million dollars. She lives in Jersey in a ten-dollar flat. She's always got more cash on hand than half a dozen business candidates for vice-president. I don't know whether she carries it in her stocking or not, but I know she's mighty popular down in the part of the town where they worship the golden calf.

"Well, about two weeks ago, Mrs. Brown stops at the door and rubbers at me for ten minutes. I'm sitting with my side to her, striking off some manifold copies of a copper-mine proposition for a nice old man from Tonopah. But I always see everything all around me. When I'm hard at work I can see things through my side combs; and I can leave one button unbuttoned in the back of my shirtwaist and see who's behind me. I didn't look around, because I make from eighteen to twenty dollars a week, and I didn't have to.

"That evening at knocking-off time she sends for me to come up to her apartment. I expected to have to typewrite about two thousand words of notes-of-hand, liens, and contracts, with a ten-cent tip in sight; but I went. Well, Man, I was certainly surprised. Old Maggie Brown had turned human.

"'Child,' says she, 'you're the most beautiful creature I ever saw in my life. I want you to quit your work and come and live with me. I've no kith or kin,' says she, 'except a husband and a son or two, and I hold no communication with any of 'em. They're extravagant burdens on a hardworking woman. I want you to be a daughter to me. They say I'm stingy and mean, and the papers print lies about my doing my own cooking and washing. It's a lie,' she goes on. 'I put my washing out, except the handkerchiefs and stockings and petticoats and collars, and light stuff like that. I've got forty million dollars in cash and stocks and bonds that are as negotiable as Standard Oil, preferred, at a church fair. I'm a lonely old woman and I need companionship. You're the most beautiful human being I ever saw,' says she. 'Will you come and live with me? I'll show 'em whether I can spend money or not,' she says.

"Well, Man, what would you have done? Of course, I fell to it. And, to tell you the truth, I began to like old Maggie. It wasn't all on account of the forty millions and what she could do for me. I was kind of lonesome in the world, too.

Everybody's got to have somebody they can explain to about the pain in their left shoulder and how fast patent-leather shoes wear out when they begin to crack. And you can't talk about such things to men you meet in hotels—they're looking for just such openings.

"So I gave up my job in the hotel and went with Mrs. Brown. I certainly seemed to have a mash on her. She'd look at me for half an hour at a time when I was sitting, reading, or looking at the magazines.

"One time I says to her: 'Do I remind you of some deceased relative or friend of your childhood, Mrs. Brown? I've noticed you give me a pretty good optical inspection from time to time.'

"'You have a face,' she says, 'exactly like a dear friend of mine—the best friend I ever had. But I like you for yourself, child, too,' she says.

"And say, Man, what do you suppose she did? Loosened up like a Marcel wave in the surf at Coney. She took me to a swell dressmaker and gave her à la carte to fit me out—money no object. They were rush orders, and madame locked the front door and put the whole force to work.

"Then we moved to—where do you think?—no; guess again—that's right—the Hotel Bonton. We had a six-room apartment; and it cost a hundred dollars a day. I saw the bill. I began to love that old lady.

"And then, Man, when my dresses began to come in—oh, I won't tell you about 'em! You couldn't understand. And I began to call her Aunt Maggie. You've read about Cinderella, of course. Well, what Cinderella said when the prince fitted that $3\frac{1}{2}$A on her foot was a hard-luck story compared to the things I told myself.

"Then Aunt Maggie says she is going to give me a coming-out banquet in the Bonton that'll make moving Vans of all the old Dutch families on Fifth Avenue.

"'I've been out before, Aunt Maggie,' says I. 'But I'll come out again. But you know,' says I, 'that this is one of the swellest hotels in the city. And you know—pardon me—that it's hard to get a bunch of notables together unless you've trained for it.

"'Don't fret about that, child,' says Aunt Maggie. 'I don't send out invitations—I issue orders. I'll have fifty guests here that couldn't be brought together again at any reception unless it were given by King Edward or William Travers Jerome. They are men, of course, and all of 'em either owe me money or intend to. Some of their wives won't come, but a good many will.'

"Well, I wish you could have been at that banquet. The dinner service was all gold and cut glass. There were about forty men and eight ladies present besides Aunt Maggie and I. You'd never have known the third richest women in the world. She had on a new black silk dress with so much passementerie on it that it sounded exactly like a hailstorm I heard once when I was staying all night with a girl that lived on a top-floor studio.

"And my dress! Say, Man, I can't waste the words on you.

It was all handmade lace—where there was any of it at all—and it cost three hundred dollars. I saw the bill. The men were all bald-headed or white side-whiskered, and they kept up a running fire of light repartee about three percent, and Bryan and the cotton crop.

"On the left of me was something that talked like a banker, and on my right was a young fellow who said he was a news-paper artist. He was the only—well, I was going to tell you.

"After the dinner was over Mrs. Brown and I went up to the apartment. We had to squeeze our way through a mob of reporters all the way through the halls. That's one of the things money does for you. Say, do you happen to know a newspaper artist named Lathrop—a tall man with nice eyes and an easy way of talking? No, I don't remember what paper he works on. Well, all right.

"When we got upstairs Mrs. Brown telephones for the bill right away. It came, and it was six hundred dollars. I saw the bill. Aunt Maggie fainted. I got her on a lounge and opened the beadwork.

"'Child,' says she, when she got back to the world, 'what was it? A raise of rent or an income tax?'

"'Just a little dinner,' says I. 'Nothing to worry about—hardly a drop in the bucket shop. Sit up and take notice—a dispossess notice, if there's no other kind.'

"But, say, Man, do you know what Aunt Maggie did? She got cold feet! She hustled me out of that Hotel Bonton at nine the next morning. We went to a rooming house on the lower West Side. She rented one room that had water on the floor below and light on the floor above. After we got moved all you could see in the room was about fifteen hundred dollars' worth of new swell dresses and a one-burner gas stove.

"Aunt Maggie had had a sudden attack of the hedges. I guess everybody has got to go on a spree once in their life. A man spends his on highballs, and a woman gets woozy on clothes. But with forty million dollars—say! I'd like to have a picture of—but, speaking of pictures, did you ever run across a newspaper artist named Lathrop—a tall—oh, I asked you that before, didn't I? He was mighty nice to me at the dinner. His voice just suited me. I guess he must have thought I was to inherit some of Aunt Maggie's money.

"Well, Mr. Man, three days of that light housekeeping was plenty for me. Aunt Maggie was affectionate as ever. She'd hardly let me get out of her sight. But let me tell you. She was a hedger from Hedgersville, Hedger County. Seventy-five cents a day was the limit she set. We cooked our own meals in the room. There I was, with a thousand dollars' worth of the latest things in clothes, doing stunts over a one-burner gas stove.

"As I say, on the third day I flew the coop. I couldn't stand for throwing together a fifteen-cent kidney stew while wearing, at the same time, a hundred-fifty-dollar housedress, with Valenciennes lace insertion. So I goes into the closet and puts on the cheapest dress Mrs. Brown had bought for me—it's the one I've got on now—not so bad for seventy-five dollars, is it? I'd left all my own clothes in my sister's flat in Brooklyn.

"'Mrs. Brown, formerly Aunt Maggie,' says I to her, 'I am going to extend my feet alternately, one after the other, in such a manner and direction that this tenement will recede from me in the quickest possible time. I am no worshiper of money,' says I, 'but there are some things I can't stand. I can stand the fabulous monster that I've read about that blows hot birds and cold bottles with the same breath. But I can't stand a quitter,' says I. 'They say you've got forty million dollars—well, you'll never have any less. And I was beginning to like you, too,' says I.

"Well, the late Aunt Maggie kicks till the tears flow. She offers to move into a swell room with a two-burner stove and running water.

"'I've spent an awful lot of money, child,' says she. 'We'll have to economize for a while. You're the most beautiful creature I ever laid eyes on,' she says, 'and I don't want you to leave me.'

"Well, you see me, don't you? I walked straight to the Acropolis and asked for my job back, and I got it. How did you say your writings were getting along? I know you've lost out some by not having me to typewrite 'em. Do you ever have 'em illustrated? And, by the way, did you ever happen to know a newspaper artist—oh, shut up! I know I asked you before. I wonder what paper he works on? It's funny, but I couldn't help thinking that he wasn't thinking about the money he might have been thinking I was thinking I'd get from old Maggie Brown. If I only knew some of the newspaper editors I'd—"

The sound of an easy footstep came from the doorway. Ida Bates saw who it was with her back hair comb. I saw her turn pink, perfect statue that she was—a miracle that I share with Pygmalion only.

"Am I excusable?" she said to me—adorable petitioner that she became. "It's—it's Mr. Lathrop. I wonder if it really wasn't the money—I wonder, if after all, he—"

Of course, I was invited to the wedding. After the ceremony I dragged Lathrop aside.

"You're an artist," said I, "and haven't figured out why Maggie Brown conceived such a strong liking for Miss Bates— that was? Let me show you."

The bride wore a simple white dress as beautifully draped as the costumes of the ancient Greeks. I took some leaves from one of the decorative wreaths in the little parlor, and made a chaplet of them, and placed them on née Bates's shining chestnut hair, and made her turn her profile to her husband.

"By jingo!" said he. "Isn't Ida's head a dead ringer for the lady's head on the silver dollar?"

THE
RANSOM
OF RED CHIEF

~~❦~~

I t looked like a good thing, but wait till I tell you. We were
down South, in Alabama—Bill Driscoll and myself—when
this kidnapping idea struck us. It was, as Bill afterward
expressed it, "during a moment of temporary mental apparition," but we didn't find that out till later.

There was a town down there, as flat as a flannel cake,
and called Summit, of course. It contained inhabitants of as
undeleterious and self-satisfied a class of peasantry as ever clus-
tered around a Maypole.

Bill and me had a joint capital of about six hundred dollars,

28

and we needed just two thousand dollars more to pull off a fraudulent town-lot scheme in Western Illinois. We talked it over on the front steps of the hotel. Philoprogenitoveness, says we, is strong in semirural communities; therefore, and for other reasons, a kidnapping project ought to do better there than in the radius of newspapers that send reporters out in plain clothes to stir up talk about such things. We knew that Summit couldn't get after us with anything stronger than con-stables and, maybe, some lackadaisical bloodhounds and a dia-tribe or two in the *Weekly Farmers' Budget*. So, it looked good.

We selected for our victim the only child of a prominent citizen named Ebenezer Dorset. The father was respectable and tight, a mortgage fancier and a stern, upright collection-plate passer and forecloser. The kid was a boy of ten, with bas-relief freckles, and hair the color of the cover of the magazine you buy at the newsstand when you want to catch a train. Bill and me figured that Ebenezer would melt down for a ransom of two thousand dollars to a cent. But wait till I tell you.

About two miles from Summit was a little mountain, cov-ered with a dense cedar brake. On the rear elevation of this mountain was a cave. There we stored provisions.

One evening after sundown, we drove in a buggy past old Dorset's house. The kid was in the street, throwing rocks at a kitten on the opposite fence.

"Hey, little boy!" says Bill. "Would you like to have a bag of candy and a nice ride!"

The boy catches Bill neatly in the eye with a piece of brick.

"That will cost the old man an extra five hundred dollars," says Bill, climbing over the wheel.

That boy put up a fight like a welterweight cinnamon bear; but, at last, we got him down in the bottom of the buggy and drove away. We took him up to the cave, and I hitched the horse in the cedar brake. After dark I drove the buggy to the little village, three miles away, where we had hired it, and walked back to the mountain.

Bill was pasting court plaster over the scratches and bruises on his features. There was a fire burning behind the big rock at the entrance of the cave, and the boy was watching a pot of boiling coffee, with two buzzard tail feathers stuck in his red hair. He points a stick at me when I come up, and says:

"Ha! Cursed paleface, do you dare to enter the camp of Red Chief, the terror of the plains?"

"He's all right now," says Bill, rolling up his trousers and examining some bruises on his shins. "We're playing Indian. We're making Buffalo Bill's show look like magic-lantern views of Palestine in the town hall. I'm Old Hank, the Trapper, Red Chief's captive, and I'm to be scalped at daybreak. By Geronimo! That kid can kick hard."

Yes, sir, that boy seemed to be having the time of his life. The fun of camping out in a cave had made him forget that he was a captive himself. He immediately christened me Snake-eye, the Spy, and announced that, when his braves returned from the warpath, I was to be broiled at the stake at the rising of the sun.

Then we had supper; and he filled his mouth full of bacon and bread and gravy, and began to talk. He made a during-dinner speech something like this:

"I like this fine. I never camped out before; but I had a pet 'possum once, and I was nine last birthday. I hate to go to school. Rats ate up sixteen of Jimmy Talbot's aunt's speckled hen's eggs. Are there any real Indians in these woods? I want some more gravy. Does the trees moving make the wind blow? We had five puppies. What makes your nose so red, Hank? My father has lots of money. Are the stars hot? I whipped Ed Walker twice, Saturday. I don't like girls. You dassent catch toads unless with a string. Do oxen make any noise? Why are oranges round? Have you got beds to sleep on in this cave? Amos Murray has got six toes. A parrot can talk, but a monkey or a fish can't. How many does it take to make twelve?"

Every few minutes he would remember that he was a pesky redskin, and pick up his stick rifle and tiptoe to the mouth of the cave to rubber for the scouts of the hated paleface. Now and then he would let out a war whoop that made Old Hank the Trapper shiver. That boy had Bill terrorized from the start.

"Red Chief," says I to the kid, "would you like to go home?"

"Aw, what for?" says he. "I don't have any fun at home. I hate to go to school. I like to camp out. You won't take me back home again, Snake-eye, will you?"

"Not right away," says I. "We'll stay here in the cave awhile."

"All right!" says he. "That'll be fine. I never had such fun in all my life."

We went to bed about eleven o'clock. We spread down some wide blankets and quilts and put Red Chief between us. We weren't afraid he'd run away. He kept us awake for three hours, jumping up and reaching for his rifle and screeching "Hist! Pard" in mine and Bill's ears, as the fancied crackle of a twig or the rustle of a leaf revealed to his young imagination the stealthy approach of the outlaw band. At last, I fell into a troubled sleep, and dreamed that I had been kidnapped and chained to a tree by a ferocious pirate with red hair.

Just at daybreak, I was awakened by a series of awful screams from Bill. They weren't yells, or howls, or shouts, or whoops, or yawps, such as you'd expect from a manly set of vocal organs—they were simply indecent, terrifying, humiliating screams, such as women emit when they see ghosts or caterpillars. It's an awful thing to hear a strong, desperate, fat man scream incontinently in a cave at daybreak.

I jumped up to see what the matter was. Red Chief was sitting on Bill's chest, with one hand twined in Bill's hair. In the other he had the sharp case knife we used for slicing bacon; and he was industriously and realistically trying to take Bill's scalp, according to the sentence that had been pronounced upon him the evening before.

The kidnapping idea struck us during a moment of temporary mental apparition.

I got the knife away from the kid and made him lie down again. But, from that moment, Bill's spirit was broken. He laid down on his side of the bed, but he never closed an eye again in sleep as long as that boy was with us. I dozed off for a while, but along toward sun-up I remembered that Red Chief had said I was to be burned at the stake at the rising of the sun. I wasn't nervous or afraid; but I sat up and lit my pipe and leaned against a rock.

"What you getting up so soon for, Sam?" asked Bill.

"Me?" says I. "Oh, I got a kind of pain in my shoulder. I thought sitting up would rest it."

"You're a liar!" says Bill. "You're afraid. You was to be burned at sunrise, and you was afraid he'd do it. And he would, too, if he could find a match. Ain't it awful, Sam? Do you think anybody will pay out money to get a little imp like that back home?"

"Sure," said I. "A rowdy kid like that is just the kind that parents dote on. Now, you and the Chief get up and cook breakfast, while I go up on the top of this mountain and reconnoiter."

I went up on the peak of the little mountain and ran my eye over the contiguous vicinity. Over towards Summit I expected to see the sturdy yeomanry of the village armed with scythes and pitchforks beating the countryside for the dastardly kidnappers. But what I saw was a peaceful landscape dotted with one man plowing with a dun mule. Nobody was dragging the creek; no couriers dashed hither and yon, bringing tidings of no news to the distracted parents. There was a sylvan attitude of somnolent sleepiness pervading that section of the external outward surface of Alabama that lay exposed to my view. "Perhaps," says I to myself, "it has not yet been discovered that the wolves have borne away the tender lambkin from the fold. Heaven help the wolves!" says I, and I went down the mountain to breakfast.

When I got to the cave I found Bill backed up against the side of it, breathing hard, and the boy threatening to smash him with a rock half as big as a coconut.

"He put a red-hot boiled potato down my back," explained Bill, "and then mashed it with his foot; and I boxed his ears. Have you got a gun about you, Sam?"

I took the rock away from the boy and kind of patched up the argument. "I'll fix you," says the kid to Bill. "No man ever yet struck the Red Chief but he got paid for it. You better beware!"

After breakfast the kid takes a piece of leather with strings wrapped around it out of his pocket and goes outside the cave unwinding it.

"What's he up to now?" says Bill, anxiously. "You don't think he'll run away, do you, Sam?"

"No fear of it," says I. "He don't seem to be much of a homebody. But we've got to fix up some plan about the ransom. There don't seem to be much excitement around Summit on account of his disappearance; but maybe they haven't realized yet that he's gone. His folks may think he's spending the night with Aunt Jane or one of the neighbors. Anyhow, he'll be missed today. Tonight we must get a message to his father demanding the two thousand dollars for his return."

Just then we heard a kind of war whoop, such as David might have emitted when he knocked out the champion Goliath. It was a sling that Red Chief had pulled out of his pocket, and he was whirling it around his head.

I dodged, and heard a heavy thud and a kind of sigh from Bill, like a horse gives out when you take his saddle off. A rock the size of an egg had caught Bill just behind his left ear. He loosened himself all over and fell in the fire across the frying pan of hot water for washing the dishes. I dragged him out and poured cold water on his head for half an hour.

By and by, Bill sits up and feels behind his ear and says: "Sam, do you know who my favorite biblical character is?"

"Take it easy," says I. "You'll come to your senses presently."

"King Herod," says he. "You won't go away and leave me here alone, will you, Sam?"

I went out and caught that boy and shook him until his freckles rattled.

"If you don't behave," says I, "I'll take you straight home. Now, are you going to be good, or not?"

"I was only funning," says he, sullenly. "I didn't mean to hurt Old Hank. But what did he hit me for? I'll behave, Snake-eye, if you won't send me home, and if you'll let me play the Black Scout today."

"I don't know the game," says I. "That's for you and Mr. Bill to decide. He's your playmate for the day. I'm going away for a while, on business. Now, you come in and make friends with him and say you are sorry for hurting him, or home you go, at once."

I made him and Bill shake hands, and then I took Bill aside and told him I was going to Poplar Grove, a little village three miles from the cave, and find out what I could about how the kidnapping had been regarded in Summit. Also, I thought it best to send a peremptory letter to old man Dorset that day, demanding the ransom and dictating how it should be paid.

"You know, Sam," says Bill, "I've stood by you without batting an eye in earthquakes, fire, and flood—in poker games, dynamite outrages, police raids, train robberies, and cyclones. I never lost my nerve yet till we kidnapped that two-legged skyrocket of a kid. He's got me going. You won't leave me long with him, will you, Sam?"

"I'll be back sometime this afternoon," says I. "You must keep the boy amused and quiet till I return. And now we'll write the letter to old Dorset."

Bill and I got paper and pencil and worked on the letter while Red Chief, with a blanket wrapped around him, strutted up and down, guarding the mouth of the cave. Bill begged me tearfully to make the ransom fifteen hundred dollars instead of

two thousand. "I ain't attempting," says he, "to decry the cele-
brated moral aspect of parental affection, but we're dealing
with humans, and it ain't human for anybody to give up two
thousand dollars for that forty-pound chunk of freckled wild-
cat. I'm willing to take a chance at fifteen hundred dollars. You
can charge the difference up to me."

So, to relieve Bill, I acceded, and we collaborated a letter
that ran this way:

Ebenezer Dorset, Esq.:

*We have your boy concealed in a place far from Summit. It is
useless for you or the most skillful detectives to attempt to find
him. Absolutely, the only terms on which you can have him
restored to you are these: We demand fifteen hundred dollars in
large bills for his return; the money to be left at midnight tonight
at the same spot and in the same box as your reply—as
hereinafter described. If you agree to these terms, send your
answer in writing by a solitary messenger tonight at half-past eight
o'clock. After crossing Owl Creek on the road to Poplar Grove,
there are three large trees about a hundred yards apart, close to
the fence of the wheat field on the right-hand side. At the bottom
of the fence post, opposite the third tree, will be found a small
pasteboard box.*

*The messenger will place the answer in this box and return
immediately to Summit.*

*If you attempt any treachery or fail to comply with our
demand as stated, you will never see your boy again.*

If you pay the money as demanded, he will be returned to

you safe and well within three hours. These terms are final, and if you do not accede to them no further communication will be attempted.

Two Desperate Men

I addressed this letter to Dorset, and put it in my pocket. As I was about to start, the kid comes up to me and says:

"Aw, Snake-eye, you said I could play the Black Scout while you was gone."

"Play it, of course," says I. "Mr. Bill will play with you. What kind of a game is it?"

"I'm the Black Scout," says Red Chief, "and I have to ride to the stockade to warn the settlers that the Indians are coming. I'm tired of playing Indian myself. I want to be the Black Scout."

"All right," says I. "It sounds harmless to me. I guess Mr. Bill will help you foil the pesky savages."

"What am I to do?" asks Bill, looking at the kid suspiciously.

"You are the hoss," says Black Scout. "Get down on your hands and knees. How can I ride to the stockade without a hoss?"

"You'd better keep him interested," said I, "till we get the scheme going. Loosen up."

Bill gets down on his all fours, and a look comes in his eye like a rabbit's when you catch it in a trap.

"How far is it to the stockade, kid?" he asks, in a husky manner of voice.

"Ninety miles," says the Black Scout. "And you have to hump yourself to get there on time. Whoa, now!"

The Black Scout jumps on Bill's back and digs his heels in his side.

"For heaven's sake," says Bill, "hurry back, Sam, as soon as you can. I wish we hadn't made the ransom more than a thousand. Say, you quit kicking me or I'll get up and warm you good."

I walked over to Poplar Grove and sat around the post office and store, talking with the chaw-bacons that came in to trade. One whiskerando says that he hears Summit is all upset on account of Elder Ebenezer Dorset's boy having been lost or stolen. That was all I wanted to know. I bought some smoking tobacco, referred casually to the price of black-eyed peas, posted my letter surreptitiously, and came away. The postmaster said the mail carrier would come by in an hour to take the mail to Summit.

When I got back to the cave Bill and the boy were not to be found. I explored the vicinity of the cave, and risked a yodel or two, but there was no response.

So I lighted my pipe and sat down on a mossy bank to await developments.

In about half an hour I heard the bushes rustle, and Bill wabbled out into the little glade in front of the cave. Behind him was the kid, stepping softly like a scout, with a broad grin on his face. Bill stopped, took off his hat, and wiped his face with a red handkerchief. The kid stopped about eight feet behind him.

"Sam," says Bill, "I suppose you'll think I'm a renegade, but I couldn't help it. I'm a grown person with masculine proclivities and habits of self-defense, but there is a time when all systems of egotism and predominance fail. The boy is gone. I sent him home. All is off. There was martyrs in old times," goes on Bill, "that suffered death rather than give up the particular graft they enjoyed. None of 'em ever was subjugated to such supernatural tortures as I have been. I tried to be faithful to our articles of depredation, but there came a limit."

"What's the trouble, Bill?" I asks him.

"I was rode," says Bill, "the ninety miles to the stockade, not barring an inch. Then, when the settlers was rescued, I was given oats. Sand ain't a palatable substitute. And then, for an hour I had to try to explain to him why there was nothin' in holes, how a road can run both ways, and what makes the grass green. I tell you, Sam, a human can only stand so much. I takes him by the neck of his clothes and drags him down the mountain. On the way he kicks my legs black and blue from the knees down; and I've got to have two or three bites on my thumb and hand cauterized.

"But he's gone"—continues Bill—"gone home. I showed him the road to Summit and kicked him about eight feet nearer there at one kick. I'm sorry we lose the ransom; but it was either that or Bill Driscoll to the madhouse."

Bill is puffing and blowing, but there is a look of ineffable peace and growing content on his rose-pink features.

"Bill," says I, "there isn't any heart disease in your family, is there?"

"No," says Bill, "nothing chronic except malaria and accidents. Why?"

"Then you might turn around," says I, "and have a look behind you."

Bill turns and sees the boy, and loses his complexion and sits down plump on the ground and begins to pluck aimlessly at grass and little sticks. For an hour I was afraid of his mind. And then I told him that my scheme was to put the whole job through immediately and that we would get the ransom and be off with it by midnight if old Dorset fell in with our proposition. So Bill braced up enough to give the kid a weak sort of smile and a promise to play the Russian in a Japanese war with him as soon as he felt a little better.

I had a scheme for collecting that ransom without danger of being caught by counterplots that ought to commend itself to professional kidnappers. The tree under which the answer was to be left—and the money later on—was close to the road fence with big, bare fields on all sides. If a gang of constables should be watching for anyone to come for the note, they could see him a long way off crossing the fields or in the road.

But no siree! At half-past eight I was up in that tree as well hidden as a tree toad, waiting for the messenger to arrive.

Exactly on time, a half-grown boy rides up the road on a bicycle, locates the pasteboard box at the foot of the fence post, slips a folded piece of paper into it, and pedals away again back toward Summit.

I waited an hour and then concluded the thing was square. I slid down the tree, got the note, slipped along the fence till I struck the woods, and was back at the cave in another half an hour. I opened the note, got near the lantern, and read it to Bill. It was written with a pen in a crabbed hand, and the sum and substance of it was this:

> *Two Desperate Men:*
>
> *Gentlemen, I received your letter today by post, in regard to the ransom you ask for the return of my son. I think you are a little high in your demands, and I hereby make you a counter-proposition, which I am inclined to believe you will accept. You bring Johnny home and pay me two hundred and fifty dollars in cash, and I agree to take him off your hands. You had better come at night, for the neighbors believe he is lost, and I couldn't be responsible for what they would do to anybody they saw bringing him back.*
>
> *Very respectfully,*
> *Ebenezer Dorset*

"Great pirates of Penzance," says I, "of all the impudent—" But I glanced at Bill, and hesitated. He had the most appealing look in his eyes I ever saw on the face of a dumb or a talking brute.

"Sam," says he, "what's two hundred and fifty dollars, after all? We've got the money. One more night of this kid will send me to a bed in Bedlam. Besides being a thorough gentleman, I think Mr. Dorset is a spendthrift for making us such a liberal offer. You ain't going to let the chance go, are you?"

"Tell you the truth, Bill," says I, "this little he ewe lamb has somewhat got on my nerves too. We'll take him home, pay the ransom, and make our getaway."

We took him home that night. We got him to go by telling him that his father had bought a silver-mounted rifle and a pair of moccasins for him, and we were to hunt bears the next day.

It was just twelve o'clock when we knocked at Ebenezer's front door. Just at the moment when I should have been abstracting the fifteen hundred dollars from the box under the tree, according to the original proposition, Bill was counting out two hundred and fifty dollars into Dorset's hand.

When the kid found out we were going to leave him at home he started up a howl like a calliope and fastened himself as tight as a leech to Bill's leg. His father peeled him away gradually, like a porous plaster.

"How long can you hold him?" asks Bill.

"I'm not as strong as I used to be," says old Dorset, "but I think I can promise you ten minutes."

"Enough," says Bill. "In ten minutes I shall cross the central, southern, and middle western states, and be legging it trippingly for the Canadian border."

And, as dark as it was, and as fat as Bill was, and as good a runner as I am, he was a good mile and a half out of Summit before I could catch up with him.

BY COURIER

I t was neither the season nor the hour when the park had frequenters; and it is likely that the young lady, who was seated on one of the benches at the side of the walk, had merely obeyed a sudden impulse to sit for a while and enjoy a foretaste of coming spring.

She rested there, pensive and still. A certain melancholy that touched her countenance must have been of recent birth, for it had not yet altered the fine and youthful contours of her cheeks, nor subdued the arch though resolute curve of her lips.

A tall young man came striding through the park along the

path near which she sat. Behind him tagged a boy carrying a suitcase. At sight of the young lady, the man's face changed to red and back to pale again. He watched her countenance as he drew nearer, with hope and anxiety mingled on his own. He passed within a few yards of her, but he saw no evidence that she was aware of his presence or existence.

Some fifty yards farther on he suddenly stopped and sat on a bench at one side. The boy dropped the suitcase and stared at him with wondering, shrewd eyes. The young man took out his handkerchief and wiped his brow. It was a good handkerchief, a good brow, and the young man was good to look at. He said to the boy:

"I want you to take a message to that young lady on that bench. Tell her I am on my way to the station, to leave for San Francisco, where I shall join that Alaska moose-hunting expedition. Tell her that, since she has commanded me neither to speak nor to write to her, I take this means of making one last appeal to her sense of justice, for the sake of what has been. Tell her that to condemn and discard one who has not deserved such treatment, without giving him her reasons or a chance to explain, is contrary to her nature as I believe it to be. Tell her that I have thus, to a certain degree, disobeyed her injunctions, in the hope that she may yet be inclined to see justice done. Go, and tell her that."

The young man dropped a half-dollar into the boy's hand. The boy looked at him for a moment with bright, canny eyes out of a dirty, intelligent face and then set off at a run. He approached the lady on the bench a little doubtfully, but unembarrassed. He touched the brim of an old plaid bicycle cap perched on the back of his head. The lady looked at him coolly, without prejudice or favor.

"Lady," he said, "dat gent on de oder bench sent yer a song and dance by me. If yer don't know de guy, and he's tryin' to do de Johnny act, say de word, and I'll call a cop in t'ree minutes. If yer does know him, and he's on de square, w'y I'll spiel yer de bunch of hot air he sent yer."

The young lady betrayed a faint interest.

"A song and dance!" she said, in a deliberate, sweet voice that seemed to clothe her words in a diaphanous garment of impalpable irony. "A new idea—in the troubadour line, I suppose. I—used to know the gentleman who sent you, so I think it will hardly be necessary to call the police. You may execute your song and dance, but do not sing too loudly. It is a little early yet for open-air vaudeville, and we might attract attention."

"Aw," said the boy, with a shrug down the length of him, "yer know what I mean, lady. 'Tain't a turn, it's wind. He told me to tell yer he's got his collars and cuffs in dat grip for a scoot clean out to 'Frisco. Den he's goin' to shoot snowbirds in de Klondike. He says you told him not to send 'round no more pink notes nor come hangin' over de garden gate, and he takes dis means of puttin' yer wise. He says yer refereed him out like

a has-been, and never give him no chance to kick at de decision. He says yer swiped him, and never said why."

The slightly awakened interest in the young lady's eyes did
not abate. Perhaps it was caused by either the originality or the
audacity of the snowbird hunter, in thus circumventing her
express commands against the ordinary modes of communication. She fixed her eye on a statue standing disconsolate in the
disheveled park, and spoke into the transmitter:

"Tell the gentleman that I need not repeat to him a description of my ideals. He knows what they have been and
what they still are. So far as they touch on this case, absolute
loyalty and truth are the ones paramount. Tell him that I have
studied my own heart as well as one can, and I know its weakness as well as I do its needs. That is why I decline to hear his
pleas, whatever they may be. I did not condemn him through
hearsay or doubtful evidence, and that is why I made no
charge. But, since he persists in hearing what he already well
knows, you may convey the matter.

"Tell him that I entered the conservatory that evening
from the rear, to cut a rose for my mother. Tell him I saw him
and Miss Ashburton beneath the pink oleander. The tableau
was pretty, but the pose and juxtaposition were too eloquent
and evident to require explanation. I left the conservatory,
and, at the same time, the rose and my ideal. You may carry
that song and dance to your impresario."

"I'm shy on one word, lady. Jux—jux—put me wise on that,
will yer?"

"Juxtaposition—or you may call it propinquity—or, if you like, being rather too near for one maintaining the position of an ideal."

The gravel spun from beneath the boy's feet. He stood by the other bench. The man's eyes interrogated him hungrily. The boy's were shining with the impersonal zeal of the translator.

"De lady says dat she's on to de fact dat gals is dead easy when a feller come spielin' ghost stories and tryin' to make up, and dat's why she won't listen to no soft soap. She says she caught yer dead to rights, huggin' a bunch o' calico in de hot-house. She sidestepped in to pull some posies and yer was squeezin' der oder gal to beat de band. She says it looked cute, all right all right, but it made her sick. She says yer better git busy, and make a sneak for de train."

The young man gave a low whistle and his eyes flashed with a sudden thought. His hand flew to the inside pocket of his coat, and drew out a handful of letters. Selecting one, he handed it to the boy, following it with a silver dollar from his vest pocket.

"Give that letter to the lady," he said, "and ask her to read it. Tell her that it should explain the situation. Tell her that, if she had mingled a little trust with her conception of the ideal, much heartache might have been avoided. Tell her that loyalty she prizes so much has never wavered. Tell her I am waiting for an answer."

The messenger stood before the lady.

"De gent says he's had de ski-bunk put on him widout no cause. He says he's no bum guy; and, lady, yer read dat letter, and I'll bet yer he's a white sport, all right."

The young lady unfolded the letter, somewhat doubtfully, and read it.

Dear Dr. Arnold:

I want to thank you for your most kind and opportune aid to my daughter last Friday evening, when she was overcome by an attack of her old heart trouble in the conservatory at Mrs. Waldron's reception. Had you not been near to catch her as she fell and to render proper attention, we might have lost her. I would be glad if you would call and undertake the treatment of her case.

Gratefully yours,
Robert Ashburton

The young lady refolded the letter, and handed it to the boy.

"De gent wants an answer," said the messenger. "What's de word?"

The lady's eyes suddenly flashed on him, bright, smiling, and wet.

"Tell that guy on the other bench," she said, with a happy, tremulous laugh, "that his girl wants him."

"De gent wants an answer."

THE
PIMIENTA
PANCAKES

‿◡⁀◠‿

W hile we were rounding up a bunch of the Triangle-O
cattle in the Frio bottoms a projecting branch of a
dead mesquite caught my wooden stirrup and gave my
ankle a wrench that laid me up in camp for a week.

On the third day of my compulsory idleness I crawled out
near the grub wagon, and reclined helpless under the con-
versational fire of Judson Odom, the camp cook. Jud was a
monologist by nature, whom Destiny, with customary blunder-
ing, had set in a profession wherein he was bereaved, for the
greater portion of his time, of an audience.

Therefore, I was manna in the desert of Jud's obmutes-cence.

Betimes I was stirred by invalid longings for something to eat that did not come under the caption of "grub." I had visions of the maternal pantry "deep as first love, and wild with all regret," and then I asked:

"Jud, can you make pancakes?"

Jud laid down his six-shooter, with which he was preparing to pound an antelope steak, and stood over me in what I felt to be a menacing attitude. He further endorsed my impression that his pose was resentful by fixing upon me with his light blue eyes a look of cold suspicion.

"Say, you," he said, with candid, though not excessive, choler, "did you mean that straight, or was you trying to throw the gaff into me? Some of the boys been telling you about me and that pancake racket?"

"No, Jud," I said, sincerely, "I meant it. It seems to me I'd swap my pony and saddle for a stack of buttered brown pan-cakes with some first crop, open kettle New Orleans sweeten-ing. Was there a story about pancakes?"

Jud was mollified at once when he saw that I had not been dealing in allusions. He brought some mysterious bags and tin boxes from the grub wagon and set them in the shade of the hackberry where I lay reclined. I watched him as he began to arrange them leisurely and untie their many strings.

"No, not a story," said Jud, as he worked, "but just the logical disclosures in the case of me and that pink-eyed snoozer from Mired Mule Cañada and Miss Willella Learight. I don't mind telling you.

"I was punching then for old Bill Toomey, on the San Miguel. One day I gets all ensnared up in aspirations for to eat some canned grub that hasn't even mooed or baaed or grunted or been in peck measures. So, I gets on my bronc and pushed the wind for Uncle Emsley Telfair's store at the Pimienta Crossing on the Neuces.

"About three in the afternoon, I throwed my bridle over a mesquite limb and walked the last twenty yards into Uncle Emsley's store. I got up on the counter and told Uncle Emsley that the signs pointed to the devastation of the fruit crop of the world. In a minute I had a bag of crackers and a long-handled spoon, with an open can each of apricots and pine-apples and cherries and greengages beside of me with Uncle Emsley busy chopping away with the hatchet at the yellow clings. I was feeling like Adam before the apple stampede, and was digging my spurs into the side of the counter and working with my twenty-four-inch spoon when I happened to look out of the window into the yard of Uncle Emsley's house, which was next to the store.

"There was a girl standing there—an imported girl with fix-ings on—philandering with a croquet maul and amusing her-self by watching my style of encouraging the fruit canning industry.

"I slid off the counter and delivered up my shovel to Uncle Emsley.

"'That's my niece,' says he; 'Miss Willella Learight, down from Palestine on a visit. Do you want that I should make you acquainted?'

"'The Holy Land,' I says to myself, my thought milling some as I tried to run 'em into the corral. 'Why not? There was sure angels in Pales— Why yes, Uncle Emsley,' I says out loud, 'I'd be awful edified to meet Miss Learight.'

"So Uncle Emsley took me out in the yard and gave us each other's entitlements.

"I never was shy about women. I never could understand why some men who can break a mustang before breakfast and shave in the dark get all left-handed and full of perspiration and excuses when they see a bolt of calico draped around what belongs in it. Inside of eight minutes me and Miss Willella was aggravating the croquet balls around as amiable as second cousins. She gave me a dig about the quantity of canned fruit I had eaten, and I got back at her, flat-footed, about how a certain lady named Eve started the fruit trouble in the first free-grass pasture—'Over in Palestine, wasn't it?' says I, as easy and pat as roping a one-year-old.

"That was how I acquired cordiality for the proximities of Miss Willella Learight; and the disposition grew larger as time passed. She was stopping at Pimienta Crossing for her health, which was very good, and for the climate, which was forty percent hotter than Palestine. I rode over to see her once every week for a while; and then I figured it out that if I doubled the number of trips I would see her twice as often.

"One week I slipped in a third trip; and that's where the pancakes and the pink-eyed snoozer busted into the game.

"That evening, while I set on the counter with a peach and two damsons in my mouth, I asked Uncle Emsley how Miss Willella was.

"'Why,' says Uncle Emsley, 'she's gone riding with Jackson Bird, the sheepman from over at Mired Mule Cañada.'

"I swallowed the peach seed and the two damson seeds. I guess somebody held the counter by the bridle while I got off; and then I walked out straight ahead till I butted against the mesquite where my roan was tied.

"'She's gone riding,' I whispered in my bronc's ear, 'with Birdstone Jack, the hired mule from Sheepman's Cañada. Did you get that, old Leather-and-Gallops?'

"That bronc of mine wept, in his way. He'd been raised a cow pony and he didn't care for snoozers.

"I went back and said to Uncle Emsley: 'Did you say a sheepman?'

"'I said a sheepman,' says Uncle again. 'You must have heard tell of Jackson Bird. He's got eight sections of grazing and four thousand head of the finest merinos south of the Arctic Circle.'

"I went out and sat on the ground in the shade of the store

and leaned against a prickly pear. I sifted sand into my boots with unthinking hands while I soliloquized a quantity about this bird with the Jackson plumage to his name.

"I never had believed in harming sheepmen. I see one, one day, reading a Latin grammar on hossback, and I never touched him! They never irritated me like they do most cow-men. You wouldn't go to work now, and impair and disfigure snoozers, would you, that eat on tables and wear little shoes and speak to you on subjects? I had always let 'em pass, just as you would a jackrabbit; with a polite word and a guess about the weather, but no stopping to swap canteens. I never thought it was worthwhile to be hostile with a snoozer. And because I'd been lenient, and let 'em live, here was one going around riding with Miss Willella Learight!

"An hour by sun they come loping back, and stopped at Uncle Emsley's gate. The sheep person helped her off; and they stood throwing each other sentences all sprightful and sagacious for a while. And then this feathered Jackson flies up in his saddle and raises his little stew pot of a hat, and trots off in the direction of his mutton ranch. By this time I had turned the sand out of my boots and unpinned myself from the prickly pear; and by the time he gets half a mile out of Pimienta, I single-foots up beside him on my bronc.

"I said that snoozer was pink-eyed, but he wasn't. His see-ing arrangement was gray enough, but his eyelashes was pink and his hair was sandy, and that gave you the idea.

"Afternoon!" says I to him.

Sheepman—he wasn't more than a lamb man, anyhow—a little thing with his neck involved in a yellow silk handkerchief, and shoes tied up in bowknots.

"'Afternoon!' says I to him. 'You now ride with a equestrian who is commonly called Dead-Moral-Certainty Judson, on account of the way I shoot. When I want a stranger to know me I always introduce myself before the draw, for I never did like to shake hands with ghosts.'

"'Ah,' says he, just like that—'Ah, I'm glad to know you, Mr. Judson. I'm Jackson Bird, from over at Mired Mule Ranch.'

"Just then one of my eyes saw a roadrunner skipping down the hill with a young tarantula in his bill, and the other eye noticed a rabbit hawk sitting on a dead limb in a water elm. I popped over one after the other with my .45 just to show him. 'Two out of three,' said I. 'Birds just naturally seem to draw my fire wherever I go.'

"'Nice shooting,' says the sheepman, without a flutter. 'But don't you sometimes ever miss the third shot? Elegant fine rain that was last week for the young grass, Mr. Judson,' says he.

"'Willie,' says I, riding over close to his palfrey, 'your infatuated parents may have denounced you by the name of Jackson, but you sure moulted into a twittering Willie—let us slough off this here analysis of rain and the elements, and get down to talk that is outside the vocabulary of parrots. That is a bad habit you have got of riding with young ladies over at Pimienta. I've known birds,' says I, 'to be served on toast for less than that. Miss Willella,' says I, 'don't ever want any nest made out of sheep's wool by a tomtit of the Jacksonian branch of ornithology. Now, are you going to quit, or do you wish for to gallop up against this Dead-Moral-Certainty attachment to my name, which is good for two hyphens and at least one set of funeral obsequies?'

"Jackson Bird flushed up some, and then he laughed.

"'Why, Mr. Judson,' says he, 'you've got the wrong idea. I've called on Miss Learight a few times; but not for the purpose you imagine. My object is purely a gastronomical one.'

"I reached for my gun.

"'Any coyote,' says I, 'that would boast of dishonorable—'

"'Wait a minute,' says this Bird, 'till I explain. What would I do with a wife? If you ever saw that ranch of mine! I do my own cooking and mending. Eating—that's all the pleasure I get out of sheep raising. Mr. Judson, did you ever taste the pancakes that Miss Learight makes?'

"'Me? No,' I told him. 'I never was advised that she was up to any culinary maneuvers.'

"'They're golden sunshine,' says he, 'honey-browned by the ambrosial fires of Epicurus. I'd give two years of my life to get the recipe for making them pancakes. That's what I went to see Miss Learight for,' says Jackson Bird, 'but I haven't been able to get it from her. It's an old recipe that's been in the family for seventy-five years. They hand it down from one generation to another, but they don't give it away to outsiders. If I could get that recipe, so I could make them pancakes for myself on my ranch, I'd be a happy man,' says Bird.

"'Are you sure,' I says to him, 'that it ain't the hand that mixes the pancakes that you're after?'

"'Sure,' says Jackson, 'Miss Learight is a mighty nice girl, but I can assure you my intentions go no further than the gas-tro'—but he seen my hand going down to my holster and he changed his similitude—'than the desire to procure a copy of the pancake recipe,' he finishes.

"'You ain't such a bad little man,' says I, trying to be fair. 'I was thinking some of making orphans of your sheep, but I'll let you fly away this time. But you stick to pancakes,' says I, 'as close as the middle one of a stack, and don't go and mistake sentiments for syrup, or there'll be singing at your ranch, and you won't hear it.'

"'To convince you that I am sincere,' says the sheepman, 'I'll ask you to help me. Miss Learight and you being closer friends, maybe she would do for you what she wouldn't for me. If you will get me a copy of that pancake recipe, I give you my word that I'll never call upon her again.'

"'That's fair,' I says, and I shook hands with Jackson Bird. 'I'll get it for you if I can, and glad to oblige.' And he turned off down the big pear flat on the Piedra, in the direction of Mired Mule, and I steered northwest for old Bill Toomey's ranch.

"It was five days afterward when I got another chance to

ride over to Pimienta. Miss Willella and me passed a gratifying evening at Uncle Emsley's. She sang some, and exasperated the piano quite a lot with quotations from the operas. I gave imitations of a rattlesnake, and told her about Snaky McFee's new way of skinning cows, and described the trip I made to Saint Louis once. We was getting along in one another's estimations fine. Thinks I, if Jackson can now be persuaded to migrate, I win. I recollect his promise about the pancake recipe, and I thinks I will persuade it from Miss Willella and give it to him; and then if I catches Birdie off of Mired Mule again, I'll make him hop the twig.

"So, along about ten o'clock, I put on a wheedling smile and says to Miss Willella: 'Now, if there's anything I do like better than the sight of a red steer on green grass it's the taste of a nice hot pancake smothered in sugarhouse molasses.'

"Miss Willella gives a little jump on the piano stool, and looked at me curious.

"'Yes,' says she, 'they're real nice. What did you say was the name of that street in Saint Louis, Mr. Odom, where you lost your hat?'

"'Pancake Avenue,' says I, with a wink, to show her that I was on about the family recipe, and couldn't be side-corralled off of the subject. 'Come now, Miss Willella,' I says; 'let's hear how you make 'em. Pancakes is just whirling in my head like wagon wheels. Start her off, now—pound of flour, eight dozen eggs, and so on. How does the catalogue of constituents run?'

"'Excuse me for a moment, please,' says Willella, and she

gives me a quick kind of sideways look, and slides off the stool. She ambled out into the other room and directly Uncle Emsley comes in in his shirtsleeves, with a pitcher of water. He turns around to get a glass on the table, and I see a .45 in his hip pocket. 'Great postholes!' thinks I, 'but here's a family thinks a heap of cooking recipes, protecting it with firearms. I've known outfits that wouldn't do that much by a family feud.'

"'Drink this here down,' says Uncle Emsley, handing me the glass of water. 'You've rid too far today, Jud, and got your-self overexcited. Try to think about something else now.'

"'Do you know how to make them pancakes, Uncle Emsley?' I asked.

"'Well, I'm not as apprised in the anatomy of them as some,' says Uncle Emsley, 'but I reckon you take a sifter of plaster of paris and a little dough and saleratus and cornmeal, and mix 'em with eggs and buttermilk as usual. Is old Bill going to ship beeves to Kansas City again this spring, Jud?'

"That was all the pancake specifications I could get that night. I didn't wonder that Jackson Bird found it uphill work. So I dropped the subject and talked with Uncle Emsley a while about hollow-horn and cyclones. And then Miss Willella came and said 'Good night,' and I hit the breeze for the ranch.

"About a week afterward I met Jackson Bird riding out of Pimienta as I rode in, and we stopped in the road for a few frivolous remarks.

"'Got the bill of particulars for them flapjacks yet?' I asked him.

"'Well, no,' says Jackson. 'I don't seem to have any success in getting hold of it. Did you try?'

"'I did,' says I, 'and 'twas like trying to dig a prairie dog out of his hole with a peanut hull. That pancake recipe must be a jooka-lorum, the way they hold on to it.'

"'I'm 'most ready to give it up,' says Jackson, so discouraged in his pronunciations that I felt sorry for him; 'but I did want to know how to make them pancakes to eat on my lonely ranch,' says he. 'I lie awake at nights thinking how good they are.'

"'You keep on trying for it,' I tells him, 'and I'll do the same. One of us is bound to get a rope over its horns before long. Well, so long, Jacksy.'

"You see, by this time we was on the peacefullest of terms. When I saw that he wasn't after Miss Willella I had more endurable contemplations of that sandy-haired snoozer. In order to help out the ambitions of his appetite I kept trying to get that recipe from Miss Willella. But every time I would say 'pancakes' she would get sort of remote and fidgety about the eye, and try to change the subject. If I held her to it she would slide out and round up Uncle Emsley with his pitcher of water and hip-pocket howitzer.

"One day I galloped over to the store with a fine bunch of blue verbenas that I cut out of a herd of wildflowers over on Poisoned Dog Prairie. Uncle Emsley looked at 'em with one eye shut and says:

"'Haven't ye heard the news?'

"'Cattle up?' I asks.

"'Willella and Jackson Bird was married in Palestine yester-day,' says he. 'Just got a letter this morning.'

"I dropped them flowers in a cracker barrel, and let the news trickle in my ears and down toward my upper left-hand shirt pocket until it got to my feet.

"'Would you mind saying that over again once more, Uncle Emsley?' says I. 'Maybe my hearing has got wrong, and you only said that prime heifers was 4.80 on the hoof, or something like that.'

"'Married yesterday,' says Uncle Emsley, 'and gone to Waco and Niagara Falls on a wedding tour. Why, didn't you see none of the signs all along? Jackson Bird has been courting Willella ever since that day he took her out riding.'

"'Then,' says I, in a kind of yell, 'what was all this zizzapa-roola he gives me about pancakes? Tell me *that*.'

"When I said 'pancakes' Uncle Emsley sort of dodged and stepped back.

"'Somebody's been dealing me pancakes from the bottom of the deck,' I says, 'and I'll find out. I believe you know. Talk up,' says I, 'or we'll mix a panful of batter right here.'

"I slid over the counter after Uncle Emsley. He grabbed at his gun, but it was in a drawer, and he missed it by two inches. I got him by the front of his shirt and shoved him in a corner.

"'Talk pancakes,' says I, 'or be made into one. Does Miss Willella make 'em?'

"'She never made one in her life and I never saw one,' says

Uncle Emsley, soothing. 'Calm down now, Jud—calm down. You've got excited, and that wound in your head is contaminating your sense of intelligence. Try not to think about pancakes.'

"'Uncle Emsley,' says I, 'I'm not wounded in the head except so far as my natural cogitative instincts run to runts. Jackson Bird told me he was calling on Miss Willella for the purpose of finding out her system of producing pancakes, and he asked me to help him get the bill of lading of the ingredients. I done so, with the results as you see. Have I been sodded down with Johnson grass by a pink-eyed snoozer, or what?'

"'Slack up your grip on my dress shirt,' says Uncle Emsley, 'and I'll tell you. Yes, it looks like Jackson Bird has gone and humbugged you some. The day after he went riding with Willella he came back and told me and her to watch out for you whenever you go to talking about pancakes. He said you was in camp once where they was cooking flapjacks, and one of the fellows cut you over the head with a frying pan. Jackson said that whenever you got overhot or excited that wound hurt you and made you kind of crazy, and you went raving about pancakes. He told us to just get you worked off of the subject and soothed down, and you wouldn't be dangerous. So, me and Willella done the best by you we knew how. Well, well,' says Uncle Emsley, 'that Jackson Bird is sure a seldom kind of a snoozer.'"

During the progress of Jud's story he had been slowly but

deftly combining certain portions of the contents of his sacks and cans. Toward the close of it he set before me the finished product—a pair of red-hot, rich-hued pancakes on a tin plate. From some secret hoarding place he also brought a lump of excellent butter and a bottle of golden syrup.

"How long ago did these things happen?" I asked him.

"Three years," said Jud. "They're living on the Mired Mule Ranch now. But I haven't seen either of 'em since. They say Jackson Bird was fixing his ranch up fine with rocking chairs and window curtains all the time he was putting me up the pancake tree. Oh, I got over it after a while. But the boys kept the racket up."

"Did you make these cakes by the famous recipe?" I asked.

"Didn't I tell you there wasn't no recipe?" said Jud. "The boys hollered pancakes till they got pancake hungry, and I cut this recipe out of a newspaper. How does the truck taste?"

"They're delicious," I answered. "Why don't you have some, too, Jud?" I was sure I heard a sigh.

"Me?" said Jud. "I don't never eat 'em."

LOST ON
DRESS PARADE

༄

Mr. Towers Chandler was pressing his evening suit in his hall bedroom. One iron was heating on a small gas stove; the other was being pushed vigorously back and forth to make the desirable crease that would be seen later on extending in straight lines from Mr. Chandler's patent-leather shoes to the edge of his low-cut vest. So much of the hero's toilet may be entrusted to our confidence. The remainder may be guessed by those whom genteel poverty has driven to ignoble expedient. Our next view of him shall be as he descends the steps of his lodging house immaculately and

72

correctly clothed; calm, assured, handsome—in appearance the typical New York young clubman setting out, slightly bored, to inaugurate the pleasures of the evening.

Chandler's honorarium was eighteen dollars per week. He was employed in the office of an architect. He was twenty-two years old; he considered architecture to be truly an art; and he honestly believed—though he would not have dared to admit it in New York—that the Flatiron Building was inferior in design to the great cathedral in Milan.

Out of each week's earnings Chandler set aside one dollar. At the end of each ten weeks, with the extra capital thus accumulated, he purchased one gentleman's evening from the bargain counter of stingy old Father Time. He arrayed himself in the regalia of millionaires and presidents; he took himself to the quarter where life is brightest and showiest, and there dined with taste and luxury. With ten dollars a man may, for a few hours, play the wealthy idler to perfection. The sum is ample for a well-considered meal, a bottle bearing a respectable label, commensurate tips, a smoke, cab fare, and the ordinary etceteras.

This one delectable evening culled from each dull seventy was to Chandler a source of renascent bliss. To the society bud comes but one debut; it stands alone sweet in her memory when her hair has whitened; but to Chandler each ten weeks brought a joy as keen, as thrilling, as new as the first had been. To sit among *bon vivants* under palms in the swirl of concealed music, to look upon the *habitués* of such a paradise and to be looked upon by them—what is a girl's first dance and short-sleeved tulle compared with this?

Up Broadway Chandler moved with the vespertine dress parade. For this evening he was an exhibit as well as a gazer. For the next sixty-nine evenings he would be dining in cheviot and worsted at dubious *table d'hôtes*, at whirlwind lunch counters, on sandwiches and beer in his hall bedroom. He was willing to do that, for he was a true son of the great city of razzle-dazzle, and to him one evening in the limelight made up for many dark ones.

Chandler protracted his walk until the forties began to intersect the great and glittering primrose way, for the evening was yet young, and when one is of the *beau monde* only one day in seventy, one loves to protract the pleasure. Eyes bright, sinister, curious, admiring, provocative, alluring were bent upon him, for his garb and air proclaimed him a devotee to the hour of solace and pleasure.

At a certain corner he came to a standstill, proposing to himself the question of turning back toward the showy and fashionable restaurant in which he usually dined on the evenings of his especial luxury. Just then a girl scuddled lightly around the corner, slipped on a patch of icy snow, and fell plump upon the sidewalk.

Chandler assisted her to her feet with instant and solicitous courtesy. The girl hobbled to the wall of the building, leaned against it, and thanked him demurely.

"I think my ankle is strained," she said. "It twisted when I fell."

"Does it pain you much?" inquired Chandler.

"Only when I rest my weight upon it. I think I will be able to walk in a minute or two."

"If I can be of any further service," suggested the young man, "I will call a cab, or—"

"Thank you," said the girl, softly but heartily. "I am sure you need not trouble yourself any further. It was so awkward of me. And my shoe heels are horridly commonsense; I can't blame them at all."

Chandler looked at the girl and found her swiftly drawing his interest. She was pretty in a refined way; and her eye was both merry and kind. She was inexpensively clothed in a plain black dress that suggested a sort of uniform such as shop girls wear. Her glossy dark-brown hair showed its coils beneath a cheap hat of black straw whose only ornament was a velvet ribbon and bow. She could have posed as a model for the self-respecting working girl of the best type.

A sudden idea came into the head of the young architect. He would ask this girl to dine with him. Here was the element that his splendid but solitary periodic feats had lacked. His brief season of elegant luxury would be doubly enjoyable if he could add to it a lady's society. This girl was a lady, he was sure—her manner and speech settled that. And in spite of her extremely plain attire he felt that he would be pleased to sit at table with her.

These thoughts passed swiftly through his mind, and he decided to ask her. It was a breach of etiquette, of course, but oftentimes wage-earning girls waived formalities in matters of this kind. They were generally shrewd judges of men; and thought better of their own judgment than they did of useless conventions. His ten dollars, discreetly expended, would enable the two to dine very well indeed. The dinner would no doubt be a wonderful experience thrown into the dull routine of the girl's life, and her lively appreciation of it would add to his own triumph and pleasure.

"I think," he said to her, with frank gravity, "that your foot needs a longer rest than you suppose. Now, I am going to suggest a way in which you can give it that and at the same time do me a favor. I was on my way to dine all by my lonely self when you came tumbling around the corner. You come with me and we'll have a cozy dinner and a pleasant talk together, and by that time your game ankle will carry you home very nicely, I am sure."

The girl looked quickly up into Chandler's clear, pleasant countenance. Her eyes twinkled once very brightly, and then she smiled ingenuously.

"But we don't know each other—it wouldn't be right, would it?" she said, doubtfully.

"There is nothing wrong about it," said the young man, candidly. "I'll introduce myself—permit me—Mr. Towers Chandler. After our dinner, which I will try to make as pleasant as possible, I will bid you good evening, or attend you safely to your door, whichever you prefer."

"But, dear me!" said the girl, with a glance at Chandler's faultless attire. "In this old dress and hat!"

"Never mind that," said Chandler, cheerfully. "I'm sure you look more charming in them than anyone we shall see in the most elaborate dinner toilette."

"My ankle does hurt yet," admitted the girl, attempting a limping step. "I think I will accept your invitation, Mr. Chandler. You may call me—Miss Marian."

"Come then, Miss Marian," said the young architect, gaily, but with perfect courtesy; "you will not have far to walk. There is a very respectable and good restaurant in the next block. You will have to lean on my arm—so—and walk slowly. It is lonely dining all by one's self. I'm just a little bit glad that you slipped on the ice."

When the two were established at a well-appointed table, with a promising waiter hovering in attendance, Chandler began to experience the real joy that his regular outing always brought to him.

The restaurant was not so showy or pretentious as the one farther down Broadway, which he always preferred, but it was nearly so. The tables were well-filled with prosperous-looking diners, there was a good orchestra, playing softly enough to make conversation a possible pleasure, and the cuisine and ser-vice were beyond criticism. His companion, even in her cheap hat and dress, held herself with an air that added distinction to the natural beauty of her face and figure. And it is certain that she looked at Chandler, with his animated but self-possessed manner and his kindling and frank blue eyes, with something not far from admiration in her own charming face.

Then it was that the Madness of Manhattan, the Frenzy of Fuss and Feathers, the Bacillus of Brag, the Provincial Plague of Pose seized upon Towers Chandler. He was on Broadway, surrounded by pomp and style, and there were eyes to look at him. On the stage of that comedy he had assumed to play the one-night part of a butterfly of fashion and an idler of means and taste. He was dressed for the part, and all his good angels had not the power to prevent him from acting it.

So he began to prate to Miss Marian of clubs, of teas, of golf and riding and kennels and cotillions and tours abroad and threw out hints of a yacht lying at Larchmont. He could see that she was vastly impressed by this vague talk, so he endorsed his pose by random insinuations concerning great wealth, and mentioned familiarly a few names that are handled reverently by the proletariat. It was Chandler's short little day, and he was wringing from it the best that could be had, as he saw it. And yet once or twice he saw the pure gold of this girl shine through the mist that his egotism had raised between him and all objects.

"This way of living that you speak of," she said, "sounds so futile and purposeless. Haven't you any work to do in the world that might interest you more?"

"My dear Miss Marian," he exclaimed—"work! Think of dressing every day for dinner, of making half a dozen calls in an afternoon—with a policeman at every corner ready to jump into your auto and take you to the station, if you get up any greater speed than a donkey cart's gait. We do-nothings are the hardest workers in the land."

The dinner was concluded, the waiter generously feed, and the two walked out to the corner where they had met. Miss Marian walked very well now; her limp was scarcely notice-able.

"Thank you for a nice time," she said, frankly. "I must run home now. I liked the dinner very much, Mr. Chandler."

He shook hands with her, smiling cordially, and said some-thing about a game of bridge at his club. He watched her for a moment, walking rather rapidly eastward, and then he found a cab to drive him slowly homeward.

In his chilly bedroom Chandler laid away his evening clothes for a sixty-nine days' rest. He went about it thought-fully.

"That was a stunning girl," he said to himself. "She's all right, too, I'd be sworn, even if she does have to work. Perhaps if I'd told her the truth instead of all that razzle-dazzle we might—but, confound it! I had to play up to my clothes."

Thus spoke the brave who was born and reared in the wig-wams of the tribe of the Manhattans.

The girl, after leaving her entertainer, sped swiftly cross-town until she arrived at a handsome and sedate mansion two squares to the east, facing on that avenue which is the high-way of Mammon and the auxiliary gods. Here she entered hurriedly and ascended to a room where a handsome young lady in an elaborate housedress was looking anxiously out the window.

"Oh, you madcap!" exclaimed the elder girl, when the other entered. "When will you quit frightening us this way? It's two hours since you ran out in that rag of an old dress and Marie's hat. Mamma has been so alarmed. She sent Louis in the auto to try to find you. You are a bad, thoughtless Puss."

The elder girl touched a button, and a maid came in a moment.

"Marie, tell Mamma that Miss Marian has returned."

"Don't scold, Sister. I only ran down to Mme. Theo's to tell her to use mauve insertion instead of pink. My costume and Marie's hat were just what I needed. Everyone thought I was a shop girl, I am sure."

"Dinner is over, dear; you stayed so late."

"I know. I slipped on the sidewalk and turned my ankle. I could not walk, so I hobbled into a restaurant and sat there until I was better. That is why I was so long."

The two girls sat in the window seat, looking out at the lights and the stream of hurrying vehicles in the avenue. The younger one cuddled down with her head in her sister's lap.

"We will have to marry someday," she said, dreamily— "both of us. We have so much money that we will not be

"Confound it! I had to play up to my clothes."

allowed to disappoint the public. Do you want me to tell you the kind of man I could love, Sis?"

"Go on, you scatterbrain," smiled the other.

"I could love a man with dark and kind blue eyes, who is gentle and respectful to poor girls, who is handsome and good and does not try to flirt. But I could love him only if he had an ambition, an object, some work to do in the world. I would not care how poor he was if I could help him build his way up. But, Sister dear, the kind of man we always meet—the man who lives an idle life between society and his clubs—I could not love a man like that, even if his eyes were blue and he were so kind to poor girls whom he met in the street."

TOMMY'S
BURGLAR

∾

At ten o'clock P.M. Felicia, the maid, left the basement door with the policeman to get a raspberry phosphate around the corner. She detested the policeman and objected earnestly to the arrangement. She pointed out, not unreasonably, that she might have been allowed to fall asleep over one of St. George Rathbone's novels on the third floor, but she was overruled. Raspberries and cops were not created for nothing.

The burglar got into the house without much difficulty; because we must have action and not too much description in a two-thousand-word story.

In the dining room he opened the slide of his dark lantern. With a brace and centerbit he began to bore into the lock of the silver closet.

Suddenly a click was heard. The room was flooded with electric light. The dark velvet portières parted to admit a fair-haired boy of eight in pink pajamas, bearing a bottle of olive oil in his hand.

"Are you a burglar?" he asked, in a sweet, childish voice.

"Listen to that," exclaimed the man, in a hoarse voice. "Am I a burglar? Wot do you suppose I have a three days' growth of bristly beard on my face for, and a cap with flaps? Give me the oil, quick, and let me grease the bit, so I won't wake up your mamma, who is lying down with a headache, and left you in charge of Felicia, who has been faithless to her trust."

"Oh, dear," said Tommy, with a sigh. "I thought you would be more up-to-date. This oil is for the salad when I bring lunch from the pantry for you. And Mamma and Papa have gone to the Metropolitan to hear De Reszke. But that isn't my fault. It only shows how long the story has been knocking around among the editors. If the author had been wise he'd have changed it to Caruso in the proofs."

"Be quiet," hissed the burglar, under his breath. "If you raise an alarm I'll wring your neck like a rabbit's."

"Like a chicken's," corrected Tommy. "You had that wrong. You don't wring rabbits' necks."

"Aren't you afraid of me?" asked the burglar.

"You know I'm not," answered Tommy. "Don't you suppose I know fact from fiction? If this wasn't a story I'd yell like an Indian when I saw you; and you'd probably tumble downstairs and get pinched on the sidewalk."

"I see," said the burglar, "that you're onto your job. Go on with the performance."

Tommy seated himself in an armchair and drew his toes up under him.

"Why do you go around robbing strangers, Mr. Burglar? Have you no friends?"

"I see what you're driving at," said the burglar, with a dark frown. "It's the same old story. Your innocence and childish insouciance is going to lead me back into an honest life. Every time I crack a crib where there's a kid around, it happens."

"Would you mind gazing with wolfish eyes at the plate of cold beef that the butler has left on the dining table?" said Tommy. "I'm afraid it's growing late."

The burglar accommodated.

"Poor man," said Tommy. "You must be hungry. If you will please stand in a listless attitude I will get you something to eat."

The boy brought a roast chicken, a jar of marmalade, and a bottle of wine from the pantry. The burglar seized a knife and fork sullenly.

"It's only been an hour," he grumbled, "since I had a lobster and a pint of musty ale up on Broadway. I wish these story

"It's mighty little I get out of these fictional jobs."

writers would let a fellow have a pepsin tablet, anyhow, between feeds."

"My papa writes books," remarked Tommy.

The burglar jumped to his feet quickly.

"You said he had gone to the opera," he hissed, hoarsely and with immediate suspicion.

"I ought to have explained," said Tommy. "He didn't buy the ticket." The burglar sat again and toyed with the wishbone.

"Why do you burgle houses?" asked the boy, wonderingly.

"Because," replied the burglar, with a sudden flow of tears. "God bless my little brown-haired boy Bessie at home."

"Ah," said Tommy, wrinkling his nose, "you got that answer in the wrong place. You want to tell your hard-luck story before you pull out the child stop."

"Oh, yes," said the burglar, "I forgot. Well, once I lived up in Milwaukee, and—"

"Take the silver," said Tommy, rising from his chair.

"Hold on," said the burglar. "But I moved away. I could find no other employment. For a while I managed to support my wife and child by passing Confederate money; but alas! I was forced to give that up because it did not belong to the Union. I became desperate and a burglar."

"Have you ever fallen into the hands of the police?" asked Tommy.

"I said 'burglar,' not 'beggar,'" answered the cracksman.

"After you finish your lunch," said Tommy, "and experience the usual change of heart, how shall we wind up the story?"

"Suppose," said the burglar, thoughtfully, "that Tony Pastor turns out earlier than usual tonight, and your father gets in from *Parsifal* at ten-thirty. I am thoroughly repentant because you have made me think of my own little boy Bessie, and—"

"Say," said Tommy, "haven't you got that wrong?"

"Not on your colored crayon drawings by B. Cory Kilvert," said the burglar. "It's always a Bessie that I have at home, artlessly prattling to the pale-cheeked burglar's bride. As I was saying, your father opens the front door just as I am departing with admonitions and sandwiches that you have wrapped up for me. Upon recognizing me as an old Harvard classmate he starts back in—"

"Not in surprise?" interrupted Tommy, with wide-open eyes.

"He starts back in the doorway," continued the burglar. And then he rose to his feet and began to shout: "Rah, rah, rah! Rah, rah, rah! Rah, rah, rah!"

"Well," said Tommy, wonderingly, "that's the first time I ever knew a burglar to give a college yell when he was burglarizing a house, even in a story."

"That's one on you," said the burglar, with a laugh. "I was practicing the dramatization. If this is put on the stage that college touch is about the only thing that will make it go."

Tommy looked his admiration.

"You're on, all right," he said.

"And there's another mistake you've made," said the burglar. "You should have gone some time ago and brought me the nine-dollar gold piece your mother gave you on your birthday to take to Bessie."

"But she didn't give it to me to take to Bessie," said Tommy, pouting.

"Come, come!" said the burglar, sternly. "It's not nice of you to take advantage because the story contains an ambiguous sentence. You know what I mean. It's mighty little I get out of these fictional jobs, anyhow. I lose all the loot, and I have to reform every time; and all the swag I'm allowed is the blamed little folderols and luck pieces that you kids hand over. Why, in one story, all I got was a kiss from a little girl who came on me when I was opening a safe. And it tasted of molasses candy, too. I've a good notion to tie this table cover over your head and keep on into the silver closet."

"Oh, no, you haven't," said Tommy, wrapping his arms around his knees. "Because if you did no editor would buy the story. You know you've got to preserve the unities."

"So've you," said the burglar, rather glumly. "Instead of sitting here talking impudence and taking the bread out of a poor man's mouth, what you'd like to be doing is hiding under the bed and screeching at the top of your voice."

"You're right, old man," said Tommy, heartily. "I wonder

what they make us do it for? I think the S.P.C.C. ought to interfere. I'm sure it's neither agreeable nor usual for a kid of my age to butt in when a full-grown burglar is at work and offer him a red sled and a pair of skates not to awaken his sick mother. And look how they make the burglars act! You'd think editors would know—but what's the use?"

The burglar wiped his hands on the tablecloth and arose with a yawn.

"Well, let's get through with it," he said. "God bless you, my little boy! You have saved a man from committing a crime this night. Bessie shall pray for you as soon as I get home and give her her orders. I shall never burglarize another house—at least not until the June magazines are out. It'll be your little sister's turn then to run in on me while I am abstracting the U.S. four percent from the tea urn and buy me off with her coral necklace and a falsetto kiss."

"You haven't got all the kicks coming to you," sighed Tommy, crawling out of his chair. "Think of the sleep I'm los-ing. But it's tough on both of us, old man. I wish you could get out of the story and really rob somebody. Maybe you'll have the chance if they dramatize us."

"Never!" said the burglar, gloomily. "Between the box office and my better impulses that your leading juveniles are supposed to awaken and the magazines that pay on publica-tion, I guess I'll always be broke."

"I'm sorry," said Tommy, sympathetically. "But I can't help

myself any more than you can. It's one of the canons of household fiction that no burglar shall be successful. The burglar must be foiled by a kid like me, or by a young lady heroine, or at the last moment by his old pal, Red Mike, who recognizes the house as one in which he used to be the coachman. You have got the worst end of it in any kind of a story."

"Well, I suppose I must be clearing out now," said the burglar, taking up his lantern and bracebit.

"You have to take the rest of this chicken and the bottle of wine with you for Bessie and her mother," said Tommy, calmly.

"But confound it," exclaimed the burglar, in an annoyed tone, "they don't want it. I've got five cases of Château de Beychsvelle at home that was bottled in 1853. That claret of yours is corked. And you couldn't get either of them to look at a chicken unless it was stewed in champagne. You know, after I get out of the story I don't have so many limitations. I make a turn now and then."

"Yes, but you must take them," said Tommy, loading his arms with the bundles.

"Bless you, young master!" recited the burglar, obedient. "Second-Story Saul will never forget you. And now hurry and let me out, kid. Our two thousand words must be nearly up."

Tommy led the way through the hall toward the front door. Suddenly the burglar stopped and called to him softly: "Ain't there a cop out there in front somewhere sparking the girl?"

"Yes," said Tommy, "but what—"

"I'm afraid he'll catch me," said the burglar. "You mustn't forget that this is fiction."

"Great head!" said Tommy, turning. "Come out by the back door."

AFTER
TWENTY YEARS

The policeman on the beat moved up the avenue impres-
sively. The impressiveness was habitual and not for show,
for spectators were few. The time was barely ten o'clock
at night, but chilly gusts of wind with a taste of rain in them
had well nigh depeopled the streets.

Trying doors as he went, twirling his club with many intri-
cate and artful movements, turning now and then to cast his
watchful eye adown the pacific thoroughfare, the officer, with
his stalwart form and slight swagger, made a fine picture of a
guardian of the peace. The vicinity was one that kept early

hours. Now and then you might see the lights of a cigar store or of an all-night lunch counter; but the majority of the doors belonged to business places that had long since been closed.

When about midway of a certain block the policeman suddenly slowed his walk. In the doorway of a darkened hardware store a man leaned, with an unlighted cigar in his mouth. As the policeman walked up to him the man spoke up quickly.

"It's all right, officer," he said, reassuringly. "I'm just waiting for a friend. It's an appointment made twenty years ago. Sounds a little funny to you, doesn't it? Well, I'll explain if you'd like to make certain it's all straight. About that long ago there used to be a restaurant where this store stands—'Big Joe' Brady's restaurant."

"Until five years ago," said the policeman. "It was torn down then."

The man in the doorway struck a match and lit his cigar. The light showed a pale, square-jawed face with keen eyes, and a little white scar near his right eyebrow. His scarfpin was a large diamond, oddly set.

"Twenty years ago tonight," said the man, "I dined here at 'Big Joe' Brady's with Jimmy Wells, my best chum, and the finest chap in the world. He and I were raised here in New York, just like two brothers, together. I was eighteen and Jimmy was twenty. The next morning I was to start for the West to make my fortune. You couldn't have dragged Jimmy out of New York; he thought it was the only place on earth.

The man in the doorway struck a match and lit his cigar.

Well, we agreed that night that we would meet here again exactly twenty years from that date and time, no matter what our conditions might be or from what distance we might have come. We figured that in twenty years each of us ought to have our destiny worked out and our fortunes made, whatever they were going to be."

"It sounds pretty interesting," said the policeman. "Rather a long time between meets, though, it seems to me. Haven't you heard from your friend since you left?"

"Well, yes, for a time we corresponded," said the other. "But after a year or two we lost track of each other. You see, the West is a pretty big proposition, and I kept hustling around over it pretty lively. But I know Jimmy will meet me here if he's alive, for he always was the truest, staunchest old chap in the world. He'll never forget. I came a thousand miles to stand in this door tonight, and it's worth it if my old partner turns up."

The waiting man pulled out a handsome watch, the lids of it set with small diamonds.

"Three minutes to ten," he announced. "It was exactly ten o'clock when we parted here at the restaurant door."

"Did pretty well out West, didn't you?" asked the policeman.

"You bet! I hope Jimmy has done half as well. He was a kind of plodder, though, good fellow as he was. I've had to compete with some of the sharpest wits going to get my pile. A man gets in a groove in New York. It takes the West to put a razor-edge on him."

The policeman twirled his club and took a step or two.

"I'll be on my way. Hope your friend comes around all right. Going to call time on him sharp?"

"I should say not!" said the other. "I'll give him half an hour at least. If Jimmy is alive on earth he'll be here by that time. So long, officer."

"Good night, sir," said the policeman, passing on along his beat, trying doors as he went.

There was now a fine, cold drizzle falling, and the wind had risen from its uncertain puffs into a steady blow. The few foot passengers astir in that quarter hurried dismally and silently along with coat collars turned high and pocketed hands. And in the door of the hardware store the man who had come a thousand miles to fill an appointment, uncertain almost to absurdity, with the friend of his youth, smoked his cigar and waited.

About twenty minutes he waited, and then a tall man in a long overcoat, with collar turned up to his ears, hurried across from the opposite side of the street. He went directly to the waiting man.

"Is that you, Bob?" he asked, doubtfully.

"Is that you, Jimmy Wells?" cried the man in the door.

"Bless my heart!" exclaimed the new arrival, grasping both the other's hands with his own. "It's Bob, sure as fate. I was certain I'd find you here if you were still in existence. Well, well, well! Twenty years is a long time. The old restaurant's gone, Bob; I wish it had lasted, so we could have had another dinner there. How has the West treated you, old man?"

"Bully; it has given me everything I asked it for. You've changed lots, Jimmy. I never thought you were so tall by two or three inches."

"Oh, I grew a bit after I was twenty."

"Doing well in New York, Jimmy?"

"Moderately. I have a position in one of the city departments. Come on, Bob; we'll go around to a place I know of, and have a good long talk about old times."

The two men started up the street, arm in arm. The man from the West, his egotism enlarged by success, was beginning to outline the history of his career. The other, submerged in his overcoat, listened with interest.

At the corner stood a drugstore, brilliant with electric lights. When they came into this glare each of them turned simultaneously to gaze upon the other's face.

The man from the West stopped suddenly and released his arm.

"You're not Jimmy Wells," he snapped. "Twenty years is a long time, but not long enough to change a man's nose from a Roman to a pug."

"It sometimes changes a good man into a bad one," said the tall man. "You've been under arrest for ten minutes, 'Silky'

Bob. Chicago thinks you may have dropped over our way and wires us she wants to have a chat with you. Going quietly, are you? That's sensible. Now, before we go to the station here's a note I was to hand to you. You may read it here at the window. It's from Patrolman Wells."

The man from the West unfolded the little piece of paper handed him. His hand was steady when he began to read, but it trembled a little by the time he had finished. The note was rather short.

Bob:
I was at the appointed place on time. When you struck the match to light your cigar I saw it was the face of the man wanted in Chicago. Somehow I couldn't do it myself, so I went around and got a plainclothes man to do the job.

Jimmy

A Double-Dyed
Deceiver

◡◠◡◠

T he trouble began in Laredo. It was the Llano Kid's fault,
for he should have confined his habit of manslaughter to
Mexicans. But the Kid was past twenty; and to have only
Mexicans to one's credit at twenty is to blush unseen on the
Rio Grande border.

It happened in old Justo Valdo's gambling house. There was
a poker game at which sat players who were not all friends, as
happens often where men ride in from afar to shoot Folly as
she gallops. There was a row over so small a matter as a pair of
queens; and when the smoke had cleared away it was found

103

that the Kid had committed an indiscretion, and his adversary had been guilty of a blunder. For the unfortunate combatant was a high-blooded youth from the cow ranches, of about the Kid's own age and possessed of friends and champions. His blunder, in missing the Kid's right ear only a sixteenth of an inch when he pulled his gun, did not lessen the indiscretion of the better marksman.

The Kid, not being equipped with a retinue, nor bountifully supplied with personal admirers and supporters—on account of a rather umbrageous reputation, even for the border—considered it not incompatible with his indisputable gameness to perform that judicious tractional act known as "pulling his freight."

Quickly the avengers gathered and sought him. Three of them overtook him within a rod of the station. The Kid turned and showed his teeth in that brilliant but mirthless smile that usually preceded his deeds of insolence and violence, and his pursuers fell back without making it necessary for him even to reach for his weapon.

But in this affair the Kid had not felt the grim thirst for encounter that usually urged him on to battle. It had been a purely chance row, born of the cards and certain epithets impossible for a gentleman to brook that had passed between the two. The Kid had rather liked the slim, haughty, brown-faced young chap whom his bullet had cut off in the first pride of manhood. And now he wanted no more blood. He wanted to get away and have a good long sleep somewhere in the sun on the mesquite grass with his handkerchief over his face. Even a Mexican might have crossed his path in safety while he was in this mood.

The Kid openly boarded the northbound passenger train that departed five minutes later. But at Webb, a few miles out, where it was flagged to take on a traveler, he abandoned that manner of escape. There were telegraph stations ahead; and the Kid looked askance at electricity and steam. Saddle and spur were his rocks of safety.

The man whom he had shot was a stranger to him. But the Kid knew that he was of the Coralitos outfit from Hidalgo; and that the punchers from that ranch were more relentless and vengeful than Kentucky feudists when wrong or harm was done to one of them. So, with the wisdom that has character-ized many great fighters, the Kid decided to pile up as many leagues as possible of chaparral and pear between himself and the retaliation of the Coralitos bunch.

Near the station was a store; and near the store, scattered among the mesquite and elms, stood the saddled horses of the customers. Most of them waited, half-asleep, with sagging limbs and drooping heads. But one, a long-legged roan with a curved neck, snorted and pawed the turf. Him the Kid mounted, gripped with his knees, and slapped gently with the owner's own quirt.

If the slaying of the temerarious cardplayer had cast a cloud over the Kid's standing as a good and true citizen, this last act of his veiled his figure in the darkest shadows of disrepute. On the Rio Grande border if you take a man's life you sometimes take trash; but if you take his horse, you take a thing the loss of which renders him poor, indeed, and which enriches you not—if you are caught. For the Kid there was no turning back now.

With the springing roan under him he felt little care or uneasiness. After a five-mile gallop he drew into the plainsman's jogging trot, and rode northeastward toward the Nueces River bottoms. He knew the country well—its most tortuous and obscure trails through the great wilderness of brush and pear, and its camps and lonesome ranches where one might find safe entertainment. Always he bore to the east; for the Kid had never seen the ocean, and he had a fancy to lay his hand upon the mane of the great Gulf, the gamesome colt of the greater waters.

So after three days he stood on the shore at Corpus Christi, and looked out across the gentle ripples of a quiet sea.

Captain Boone, of the schooner *Flyaway*, stood near his skiff, which one of his crew was guarding in the surf. When ready to sail he had discovered that one of the necessaries of life, in the parallelogrammatic shape of plug tobacco, had been forgotten. A sailor had been dispatched for the missing cargo. Meanwhile the captain paced the sands, chewing profanely at his pocket store.

A slim, wiry youth in high-heeled boots came down to the water's edge. His face was boyish, but with a premature severity that hinted at a man's experience. His complexion was naturally dark; and the sun and wind of an outdoor life had burned it to a coffee brown. His hair was as black and straight as an Indian's; his face had not yet been upturned to the humiliation of a razor; his eyes were a cold and steady blue. He carried his left arm somewhat away from his body, for pearl-handled .45s are frowned upon by town marshals, and are a little bulky when packed in the left armhole of one's vest. He looked beyond Captain Boone at the gulf with the impersonal and expressionless dignity of a Chinese emperor.

"Thinkin' of buyin' that 'ar gulf, buddy?" asked the captain, made sarcastic by his narrow escape from the tobaccoless voyage.

"Why, no," said the Kid gently, "I reckon not. I never saw it before. I was just looking at it. Not thinking of selling it, are you?"

"Not this trip," said the captain. "I'll send it to you C.O.D. when I get back to Buenas Tierras. Here comes that capstan-footed lubber with the chewin'. I ought to've weighed anchor an hour ago."

"Is that your ship out there?" asked the Kid.

"Why, yes," answered the captain, "if you want to call a schooner a ship, and I don't mind lyin'. But you better say Miller and Gonzales, owners, and ordinary plain, Billy-be-damned old Samuel K. Boone, skipper."

"Where are you going to?" asked the refugee.

"Buenas Tierras, coast of South America—I forget what they called the country the last time I was there. Cargo—lumber, corrugated iron, and machetes."

"What kind of a country is it?" asked the Kid. "Hot or cold?"

"Warmish, buddy,".said the captain. "But a regular Paradise Lost for elegance of scenery and be-yooty of geography. Ye're wakened every morning by the sweet singin' of red birds with seven purple tails, and the sighin' of breezes in the posies and roses. And the inhabitants never work, for they can reach out and pick steamer baskets of the choicest hothouse fruit without gettin' out of bed. And there's no Sunday and no ice and no rent and no troubles and no use and no nothin'. It's a great country for a man to go to sleep with, and wait for somethin' to turn up. The bananys and oranges and hurricane and pineapples that ye eat comes from there."

"That sounds to me!" said the Kid, at last betraying interest. "What'll the expressage be to take me out there with you?"

"Twenty-four dollars," said Captain Boone; "grub and transportation. Second cabin. I haven't got a first cabin."

"You've got my company," said the Kid, pulling out a buckskin bag.

With three hundred dollars he had gone to Laredo for his regular "blowout." The duel in Valdos's had cut short his season of hilarity, but it had left him with nearly two hundred dollars for aid in the flight that it had made necessary.

"All right, buddy," said the captain. "I hope your ma won't blame me for this little childish escapade of yours." He beckoned to one of the boat's crew. "Let Sanchez lift you out to the skiff so you won't get your feet wet."

Thacker, the United States consul at Buenas Tierras, was not yet drunk. It was only eleven o'clock; and he never arrived at his desired state of beatitude—a state where he sang ancient maudlin vaudeville songs and pelted his screaming parrot with banana peels—until the middle of the afternoon. So, when he looked up from his hammock at the sound of a slight cough, and saw the Kid standing in the door of the consulate, he was still in a condition to extend the hospitality and courtesy due from the representative of a great nation. "Don't disturb yourself," said the Kid easily. "I just dropped in. They told me it was customary to light at your camp before starting in to round up the town. I just came in on a ship from Texas."

"Glad to see you, Mr.—," said the consul.

The Kid laughed.

"Sprague Dalton," he said. "It sounds funny to me to hear it. I'm called the Llano Kid in the Rio Grande country."

"I'm Thacker," said the consul. "Take that cane-bottom chair. Now if you've come to invest, you want somebody to advise you. These people will cheat you out of the gold in your teeth if you don't understand their ways. Try a cigar?"

"Much obliged," said the Kid, "but if it wasn't for my corn shucks and the little bag in my back pocket I couldn't live a minute." He took out his "makings," and rolled a cigarette.

"They speak Spanish here," said the consul. "You'll need an interpreter. If there's anything I can do, why, I'd be delighted. If you're buying fruit lands or looking for a concession of any sort, you'll want somebody who knows the ropes to look out for you."

"I speak Spanish," said the Kid, "about nine times better than I do English. Everybody speaks it on the range where I come from. And I'm not in the market for anything."

"You speak Spanish?" said Thacker, thoughtfully. He regarded the Kid absorbedly.

"You look like a Spaniard, too," he continued. "And you're from Texas. And you can't be more than twenty or twenty-one. I wonder if you've got any nerve."

"You got a deal of some kind to put through?" asked the Texan, with unexpected shrewdness.

"Are you open to a proposition?" said Thacker.

"What's the use to deny it?" said the Kid. "I got into a little gun frolic down in Laredo, and plugged a white man. There wasn't any Mexican handy. And I come down to your parrot-and-money range just for to smell the morning glories and marigolds. Now, do you *sabe?*"

Thacker got up and closed the door.

"Let me see your hand," he said.

He took the Kid's left hand, and examined the back of it closely.

"I can do it," he said, excitedly. "Your flesh is as hard as wood and as healthy as a baby's. It will heal in a week."

"If it's a fistfight you want to back me for," said the Kid, "don't put your money up yet. Make it gun work, and I'll keep you company. But no bare-handed scrapping, like ladies at a tea party, for me."

"It's easier than that," said Thacker. "Just step here, will you?"

Through the window he pointed to a two-story white-stuccoed house with wide galleries rising amid the deep-green tropical foliage on a wooden hill that sloped gently from the sea.

"In that house," said Thacker, "a fine old Castilian gentle-man and his wife are yearning to gather you into their arms and fill your pockets with money. Old Santos Urique lives there. He owns half the gold mines in the country."

"You haven't been eating loco weed, have you?" asked the Kid.

"Sit down again," said Thacker, "and I'll tell you. Twelve years ago they lost a kid. No, he didn't die—although most of 'em here do from drinking the surface water. He was a wild lit-tle devil, even if he wasn't but eight years old. Everybody knows about it. Some Americans who were through here prospecting for gold had letters to Señor Urique, and the boy was a favorite with them. They filled his head with big stories about the States; and about a month after they left, the kid disappeared, too. He was supposed to have stowed himself away among the banana bunches on a fruit steamer, and gone to New Orleans. He was seen once afterward in Texas, it was thought, but they never heard anything more of him. Old Urique has spent thousands of dollars having him looked for. The madam was broken up worst of all. The kid was her life. She wears mourning yet. But they say she believes he'll come back to her someday, and never gives up hope. On the back of the boy's left hand was tattooed a flying eagle carrying a spear in his claws. That's old Urique's coat of arms or something that he inherited in Spain."

The Kid raised his left hand slowly and gazed at it curiously.

"That's it," said Thacker, reaching behind the official desk for his bottle of smuggled brandy. "You're not so slow. I can do it. What was I consul at Sandakan for? I never knew till now. In a week I'll have the eagle bird with the frog sticker blended in so you'd think you were born with it. I brought a set of the needles and ink just because I was sure you'd drop in someday, Mr. Dalton."

"Oh, hell," said the Kid. "I thought I told you my name!"

"All right, 'Kid,' then. It won't be that long. How does 'Señorito Urique' sound, for a change?"

"I never played son any that I remember of," said the Kid.

The Kid raised his left hand slowly and gazed at it curiously.

"If I had any parents to mention they went over the divide about the time I gave my first bleat. What is the plan of your roundup?"

Thacker leaned back against the wall and held his glass up to the light.

"We've come now," said he, "to the question of how far you're willing to go in a little matter of the sort."

"I told you why I came down here," said the Kid simply.

"A good answer," said the consul. "But you won't have to go that far. Here's the scheme. After I get the trademark tattooed on your hand I'll notify old Urique. In the meantime I'll furnish you with all of the family history I can find out, so you can be studying up points to talk about. You've got the looks, you speak the Spanish, you know the facts, you can tell about Texas, you've got the tattoo mark. When I notify them that the rightful heir has returned and is waiting to know whether he will be received and pardoned, what will happen? They'll simply rush down here and fall on your neck, and the curtain goes down for refreshments and a stroll in the lobby."

"I'm waiting," said the Kid. "I haven't had my saddle off in your camp long, pardner, and I never met you before; but if you intend to let it go at a parental blessing, why, I'm mistaken in my man, that's all."

"Thanks," said the consul. "I haven't met anybody in a long time that keeps up with an argument as well as you do. The rest of it is simple. If they take you in only for a while it's

long enough. Don't give 'em time to hunt up the strawberry
mark on your left shoulder. Old Urique keeps anywhere from
fifty thousand to a hundred thousand dollars in his house all
the time in a little safe that you could open with a shoe but-
toner. Get it. My skill as a tattooer is worth half the boodle.
We go halves and catch a tramp steamer for Rio de Janeiro.
Let the United States go to pieces if it can't get along without
my services. *Qué dice, señor?*"

"It sounds to me!" said the Kid, nodding his head. "I'm out
for the dust."

"All right, then," said Thacker. "You'll have to keep close
until we get the bird on you. You can live in the back room
here. I do my own cooking, and I'll make you as comfortable as
a parsimonious government will allow me."

Thacker had set the time at a week, but it was two weeks
before the design that he patiently tattooed upon the Kid's
hand was to his notion. And then Thacker called a *muchacho*,
and dispatched this note to the intended victim:

El Señor Don Santos Urique
La Casa Blanca

My Dear Sir,
I beg permission to inform you that there is in my house as a
temporary guest a young man who arrived in Buenas Tierras
from the United States some days ago. Without wishing to excite
any hopes that may not be realized, I think there is a possibility of

*his being your long-absent son. It might be well for you to call
and see him. If he is, it is my opinion that his intention was to
return to his home, but upon arriving here, his courage failed him
from doubts as to how he would be received.*

Your true servant,
Thompson Thacker

Half an hour afterward—quick time for Buenas Tierras—
Señor Urique's ancient landau drove to the consul's door, with
the barefooted coachman beating and shouting at the team of
fat, awkward horses.

A tall man with a white mustache alighted, and assisted to
the ground a lady who was dressed and veiled in unrelieved
black.

The two hastened inside, and were met by Thacker with
his best diplomatic bow. By his desk stood a slender young man
with clear-cut, sun-browned features and smoothly brushed
black hair.

Señora Urique threw back her heavy veil with a quick gesture. She was past middle age, and her hair was beginning to
silver, but her full, proud figure and clear olive skin retained
traces of the beauty peculiar to the Basque province. But, once
you had seen her eyes, and comprehended the great sadness
that was revealed in their deep shadows and hopeless expression, you saw that the woman lived only in some memory.

She bent upon the young man a long look of the most ago-
nized questioning. Then her great black eyes turned, and her

gaze rested upon his left hand. And then with a sob, not loud, but seeming to shake the room, she cried *"Hijo mio!"* and caught the Llano Kid to her heart.

A month afterward the Kid came to the consulate in response to a message sent by Thacker.

He looked the young Spanish caballero. His clothes were imported, and the wiles of the jewelers had not been spent upon him in vain. A more than respectable diamond shone on his finger as he rolled a shuck cigarette.

"What's doing?" asked Thacker.

"Nothing much," said the Kid calmly. "I eat my first iguana steak today. They're them big lizards, you *sabe?* I reckon, though, that frijoles and side bacon would do me about as well. Do you care for iguanas, Thacker?"

"No, nor for some other kinds of reptiles," said Thacker.

It was three in the afternoon, and in another hour he would be in his state of beatitude.

"It's time you were making good, sonny," he went on, with an ugly look on his reddened face. "You're not playing up to me square. You've been the prodigal son for four weeks now, and you could have had veal for every meal on a gold dish if you'd wanted it. Now, Mr. Kid, do you think it's right to leave me out so long on a husk diet? What's the trouble? Don't you get your filial eyes on anything that looks like cash in the Casa Blanca? Don't tell me you don't. Everybody knows where old

Urique keeps his stuff. It's U.S. currency, too; he don't accept anything else. What's doing? Don't say 'nothing' this time."

"Why, sure," said the Kid, admiring his diamond, "there's plenty of money up there. I'm no judge of collateral in bunches, but I will undertake for to say that I've seen the rise of fifty thousand dollars at a time in that tin grub box that my adopted father calls his safe. And he lets me carry the key sometimes just to show me that he knows I'm the real little Francisco that strayed from the herd a long time ago."

"Well, what are you waiting for?" asked Thacker angrily. "Don't you forget that I can upset your applecart any day I want to. If old Urique knew you were an impostor, what sort of things would happen to you? Oh, you don't know this country, Mr. Texas Kid. The laws here have got mustard spread between 'em. These people here'd stretch you out like a frog that had been stepped on, and give you about fifty sticks at every corner of the plaza. And they'd wear every stick out, too. What was left of you they'd feed to alligators."

"I might as well tell you now, pardner," said the Kid, sliding down low on his steamer chair, "that things are going to stay just as they are. They're about right now."

"What do you mean?" asked Thacker, rattling the bottom of his glass on his desk.

"The scheme's off," said the Kid. "And whenever you have the pleasure of speaking to me address me as Don Francisco Urique. I'll guarantee I'll answer to it. We'll let Colonel

Urique keep his money. His little tin safe is as good as the time locker in the First National Bank of Laredo as far as you and me are concerned."

"You're going to throw me down, then, are you?" said the consul.

"Sure," said the Kid, cheerfully. "Throw you down. That's it. And now I'll tell you why. The first night I was up at the colonel's house they introduced me to a bedroom. No blankets on the floor—a real room, with a bed and things in it. And before I was asleep, in comes this artificial mother of mine and tucks in the covers. 'Panchito,' she says, 'my little lost one, God has brought you back to me. I bless His name forever.' It was that, or some truck like that, she said. And down comes a drop or two of rain and hits me on the nose. And all that stuck by me, Mr. Thacker. And it's been that way ever since. And it's got to stay that way. Don't you think that it's for what's in it for me, either, that I say so. If you have any such ideas keep 'em to yourself. I haven't had much truck with women in my life, and no mothers to speak of, but here's a lady that we've got to keep fooled. Once she stood it; twice she won't. I'm a low-down wolf, and the devil may have sent me on this trail instead of God, but I'll travel it to the end. And now, don't forget that I'm Don Francisco Urique whenever you happen to mention my name."

"I'll expose you today, you—you double-eyed traitor," stammered Thacker.

The Kid arose and, without violence, took Thacker by the throat with a hand of steel, and shoved him slowly into a corner. Then he drew from under his left arm his pearl-handled .45 and poked the cold muzzle of it against the consul's mouth.

"I told you why I come here," he said, with his old freezing smile. "If I leave here, you'll be the reason. Never forget it, pardner. Now, what is my name?"

"Er—Don Francisco Urique," gasped Thacker.

From outside came a sound of wheels, and the shouting of someone, and the sharp thwacks of a wooden whipstock upon the backs of fat horses.

The Kid put up his gun, and walked toward the door. But he turned again and came back to the trembling Thacker, and held up his left hand with its back toward the consul.

"There's one more reason," he said, slowly, "why things have got to stand as they are. The fellow I killed in Laredo had one of them same pictures on his left hand."

Outside, the ancient landau of Don Santos Urique rattled to the door. The coachman ceased his bellowing. Señora Urique, in a voluminous gay gown of white lace and flying ribbons, leaned forward with a happy look in her great soft eyes.

"Are you within, dear son?" she called, in the rippling Castilian.

"*Madre mía, yo vengo* [Mother, I come]," answered the young Don Francisco Urique.

GIRL

～♪～

In gilt letters on the ground glass of the door of room No. 962 were the words: "Robbins & Hartley, Brokers." The clerks had gone. It was past five, and with the solid tramp of a drove of prize Percherons, scrubwomen were invading the cloud-capped twenty-story office building. A puff of red-hot air flavored with lemon peelings, soft-coal smoke, and train oil came in through the half-open windows.

Robbins, fifty, something of an overweight beau, and addicted to first nights and hotel palm rooms, pretended to be envious of his partner's commuter's joys.

"Going to be something doing in the humidity line

tonight," he said. "You out-of-town chaps will be the people, with your katydids and moonlight and long drinks and things out on the front porch."

Hartley, twenty-nine, serious, thin, good-looking, nervous, sighed and frowned a little.

"Yes," said he, "we always have cool nights in Floralhurst, especially in the winter."

A man with an air of mystery came in the door and went up to Hartley.

"I've found where she lives," he announced in the portentous half-whisper that makes the detective at work a marked being to his fellow men.

Hartley scowled him into a state of dramatic silence and quietude. But by that time Robbins had got his cane and set his tiepin to his liking, and with a debonair nod went out to his metropolitan amusements.

"Here is the address," said the detective in a natural tone, being deprived of an audience to foil.

Hartley took the leaf torn out of the sleuth's dingy memorandum book. On it were penciled the words "Vivienne Arlington, No. 341 East —th Street, care of Mrs. McComus."

"Moved there a week ago," said the detective. "Now, if you want any shadowing done, Mr. Hartley, I can do you as fine a job in that line as anybody in the city. It will be only seven dollars a day and expenses. Can send in a daily typewritten report, covering—"

"You needn't go on," interrupted the broker. "It isn't a case of that kind. I merely wanted the address. How much shall I pay you?"

"One day's work," said the sleuth. "A tenner will cover it."

Hartley paid the man and dismissed him. Then he left the office and boarded a Broadway car. At the first large crosstown artery of travel he took an eastbound car that deposited him in a decaying avenue, whose ancient structures once sheltered the pride and glory of the town.

Walking a few squares, he came to the building that he sought. It was a new flat-house, bearing carved upon its cheap stone portal its sonorous name, "The Vallambrosa." Fire escapes zigzagged down its front—these laden with household goods, drying clothes, and squalling children evicted by the midsummer heat. Here and there a pale rubber plant peeped from the miscellaneous mass as if wondering to what kingdom it belonged—vegetable, animal, or artificial.

Hartley pressed the "McComus" button. The door latch clicked spasmodically—now hospitably, now doubtfully, as though in anxiety whether it might be admitting friends or duns. Hartley entered and began to climb the stairs after the manner of those who seek their friends in city flat-houses— which is the manner of a boy who climbs an apple tree, stopping when he comes upon what he wants.

On the fourth floor he saw Vivienne standing in an open door. She invited him inside, with a nod and a bright, genuine smile. She placed a chair for him near a window, and poised herself gracefully upon the edge of one of those Jekyll-and-Hyde pieces of furniture that are masked and mysteriously hooded, unguessable bulks by day and inquisitorial racks of torture by night.

Hartley cast a quick, critical, appreciative glance at her before speaking, and told himself that his taste in choosing had been flawless.

Vivienne was about twenty-one. She was of the purest Saxon type. Her hair was a ruddy golden, each filament of the neatly gathered mass shining with its own luster and delicate graduation of color. In perfect harmony were her ivory-clear complexion and deep sea-blue eyes that looked upon the world with the ingenuous calmness of a mermaid or the pixie of an undiscovered mountain stream. Her frame was strong and yet possessed the grace of absolute naturalness. And yet with all her Northern clearness and frankness of line and coloring, there seemed to be something of the tropics in her—something of languor in the droop of her pose, of love of ease in her ingenuous complacency of satisfaction and comfort in the mere act of breathing—something that seemed to claim for her a right as a perfect work of nature to exist and be admired equally with a rare flower or some beautiful, milk-white dove among its sober-hued companions.

She was dressed in a white waist and dark skirt—the discreet masquerade of goose girl and duchess.

"Vivienne," said Hartley, looking at her pleadingly, "you

did not answer my last letter. It was only by nearly a week's search that I found where you had moved to. Why have you kept me in suspense when you knew how anxiously I was waiting to see you and hear from you?"

The girl looked out the window dreamily.

"Mr. Hartley," she said hesitatingly, "I hardly know what to say to you. I realize all the advantages of your offer, and sometimes I feel sure that I could be contented with you. But, again, I am doubtful. I was born a city girl, and I am afraid to bind myself to a quiet suburban life."

"My dear girl," said Hartley, ardently, "have I not told you that you shall have everything that your heart can desire that is in my power to give you? You shall come to the city for the theaters, for shopping, and to visit your friends as often as you care to. You can trust me, can you not?"

"To the fullest," she said, turning her frank eyes upon him with a smile. "I know you are the kindest of men, and that the girl you get will be a lucky one. I learned all about you when I was at the Montgomerys'."

"Ah!" exclaimed Hartley, with a tender, reminiscent light in his eye. "I remember well the evening I first saw you at the Montgomerys'. Mrs. Montgomery was sounding your praises to me all the evening. And she hardly did you justice. I shall never forget that supper. Come, Vivienne, promise me. I want you. You'll never regret coming with me. No one else will ever give you as pleasant a home."

The girl sighed and looked down at her folded hands.

A sudden jealous suspicion seized Hartley.

"Tell me, Vivienne," he asked, regarding her keenly, "is there another—is there someone else?"

A rosy flush crept slowly over her fair cheeks and neck.

"You shouldn't ask that, Mr. Hartley," she said, in some confusion. "But I will tell you. There is one other—but he has no right—I have promised him nothing."

"His name?" demanded Hartley, sternly.

"Townsend."

"Rafford Townsend!" exclaimed Hartley, with a grim tightening of his jaw. "How did that man come to know you? After all I've done for him—"

"His auto has just stopped below," said Vivienne, bending over the windowsill. "He's coming for his answer. Oh, I don't know what to do!"

The bell in the flat kitchen whirred. Vivienne hurried to press the latch button.

"Stay here," said Hartley. "I will meet him in the hall."

Townsend, looking like a Spanish grandee in his light tweeds, panama hat, and curling black mustache, came up the stairs three at a time. He stopped at sight of Hartley and looked foolish.

"Go back," said Hartley, firmly, pointing downstairs with his forefinger.

"Hullo!" said Townsend, feigning surprise. "What's up? What are you doing here, old man?"

"Go back," repeated Hartley, inflexibly. "The Law of the

Jungle. Do you want the Pack to tear you to pieces? The kill is mine."

"I came here to see a plumber about the bathroom connections," said Townsend, bravely.

"All right," said Hartley. "You shall have that lying plaster to stick upon your traitorous soul. But, go back."

Townsend went downstairs, leaving a bitter word to be wafted up the draft of the staircase. Hartley went back to his wooing.

"Vivienne," said he, masterfully. "I have got to have you. I will take no more refusals or dillydallying."

"When do you want me?" she asked.

"Now. As soon as you can get ready."

She stood calmly before him and looked him in the eye.

"Do you think for one moment," she said, "that I would enter your home while Heloise is there?"

Hartley cringed as if from an unexpected blow. He folded his arms and paced the carpet once or twice.

"She shall go," he declared, grimly. Drops stood upon his brow. "Why should I let that woman make my life miserable? Never have I seen one day of freedom from trouble since I have known her. You are right, Vivienne. Heloise must be sent away before I can take you home. But she shall go. I have decided. I will turn her from my doors."

"When will you do this?" asked the girl.

Hartley clenched his teeth and bent his brows together.

"Go back. The kill is mine."

"Tonight," he said, resolutely. "I will send her away tonight."

"Then," said Vivienne, "my answer is 'yes.' Come for me when you will."

She looked into his eyes with a sweet, sincere light in her own. Hartley could scarcely believe that her surrender was true, it was so swift and complete.

"Promise me," he said, feelingly, "on your word and honor."

"On my word and honor," repeated Vivienne, softly.

At the door he turned and gazed at her happily, but yet as one who scarcely trusts the foundations of his joy.

"Tomorrow," he said, with a forefinger of reminder uplifted.

"Tomorrow," she repeated with a smile of truth and candor.

In an hour and forty minutes Hartley stepped off the train at Floralhurst. A brisk walk of ten minutes brought him to the gate of a handsome two-story cottage set upon a wide and well-tended lawn. Halfway to the house he was met by a woman with jet-black braided hair and flowing white summer gown, who half-strangled him without apparent cause.

When they stepped into the hall she said:

"Mamma's here. The auto is coming for her in half an hour. She came to dinner, but there's no dinner."

"I've something to tell you," said Hartley. "I thought to break it to you gently, but since your mother is here we may as well out with it."

He stooped and whispered something at her ear.

His wife screamed. Her mother came running into the hall. The dark-haired woman screamed again—the joyful scream of a well-beloved and petted woman.

"Oh, Mamma!" she cried, ecstatically. "What do you think? Vivienne is coming to cook for us! She is the one that stayed with the Montgomerys a whole year. And now, Billy, dear," she concluded, "you must go right down into the kitchen and discharge Heloise. She has been drunk again the whole day long."

A
CHAPARRAL
CHRISTMAS GIFT

～⁀ ⁀～

The original cause of the trouble was about twenty years in growing.

At the end of that time it was worth it.

Had you lived anywhere within fifty miles of Sundown Ranch you would have heard of it. It possessed a quantity of jet-black hair, a pair of extremely frank, deep-brown eyes, and a laugh that rippled across the prairie like the sound of a hidden brook. The name of it was Rosita McMullen; and she was the daughter of old man McMullen of the Sundown Sheep Ranch.

There came riding on red roan steeds—or, to be more

133

explicit, on a paint and a flea-bitten sorrel—two wooers. One was Madison Lane, and the other was the Frio Kid. But at that time they did not call him the Frio Kid, for he had not earned the honors of special nomenclature. His name was simply Johnny McRoy.

It must not be supposed that these two were the sum of the agreeable Rosita's admirers. The broncos of a dozen others champed their bits at the long hitching rack of the Sundown Ranch. Many were the sheeps' eyes that were cast in those savannas that did not belong to the flocks of Dan McMullen. But of all the cavaliers, Madison Lane and Johnny McRoy galloped far ahead, wherefore they are to be chronicled.

Madison Lane, a young cattleman from the Nueces country, won the race. He and Rosita were married one Christmas day. Armed, hilarious, vociferous, magnanimous, the cowmen and the sheepmen, laying aside their hereditary hatred, joined forces to celebrate the occasion.

Sundown Ranch was sonorous with the cracking of jokes and six-shooters, the shine of buckles and bright eyes, the outspoken congratulations of the herders of kine.

But while the wedding feast was at its liveliest there descended upon it Johnny McRoy, bitten by jealousy, like one possessed.

"I'll give you a Christmas present," he yelled shrilly at the door, with his .45 in his hand. Even then he had some reputation as an offhand shot.

His first bullet cut a neat underbit in Madison Lane's right ear. The barrel of his gun moved an inch. The next shot would have been the bride's had not Carson, a sheepman, possessed a mind with triggers somewhat well oiled and in repair. The guns of the wedding party had been hung, in their belts, upon nails in the wall when they sat at table, as a concession to good taste. But Carson, with great promptness, hurled his plate of roast venison and frijoles at McRoy, spoiling his aim. The second bullet, then, only shattered the white petals of a Spanish dagger flower suspended two feet above Rosita's head.

The guests spurned their chairs and jumped for their weapons. It was considered an improper act to shoot the bride and groom at a wedding. In about six seconds there were twenty or so bullets due to be whizzing in the direction of Mr. McRoy.

"I'll shoot better next time," yelled Johnny; "and there'll be a next time." He backed rapidly out of the door.

Carson, the sheepman, spurred on to attempt further exploits by the success of his plate throwing, was first to reach the door. McRoy's bullet from the darkness laid him low.

The cattlemen then swept out upon him, calling for vengeance, for, while the slaughter of a sheepman has not always lacked condonement, it was a decided misdemeanor in this instance. Carson was innocent; he was no accomplice at the matrimonial proceedings; nor had anyone heard him quote the line "Christmas comes but once a year" to the guests.

But the sortie failed in its vengeance. McRoy was on his horse and away, shouting back curses and threats as he galloped into the concealing chaparral.

That night was the birth night of the Frio Kid. He became the "bad man" of that portion of the state. The rejection of his suit by Miss McMullen turned him to a dangerous man. When officers went after him for the shooting of Carson, he killed two of them, and entered upon the life of an outlaw. He became a marvelous shot with either hand. He would turn up in towns and settlements, raise a quarrel at the slightest opportunity, pick off his man, and laugh at the officers of the law. He was so cool, so deadly, so rapid, so inhumanly bloodthirsty that none but faint attempts were ever made to capture him. When he was at last shot and killed by a little one-armed Mexican who was nearly dead himself from fright, the Frio Kid had the deaths of eighteen men on his head. About half of these were killed in fair duels depending upon the quickness of the draw. The other half were men whom he assassinated from absolute wantonness and cruelty.

Many tales are told along the border of his impudent courage and daring. But he was not one of the breed of desperadoes who have seasons of generosity and even of softness. They say he never had mercy on the object of his anger. Yet at this and every Christmastide it is well to give each one credit, if it can be done, for whatever speck of good he may have possessed. If the Frio Kid ever did a kindly act or felt a throb of generosity in his heart it was once at such a time and season, and this is the way it happened.

One who has been crossed in love should never breathe the odor of the blossoms of the ratama tree. It stirs the memory to a dangerous degree.

One December in the Frio country there was a ratama tree in full bloom, for the winter had been as warm as springtime. That way rode the Frio Kid and his satellite and co-murderer, Mexican Frank. The Kid reined in his mustang, and sat in his saddle, thoughtful and grim, with dangerously narrowing eyes. The rich, sweet scent touched him somewhere beneath his ice and iron.

"I don't know what I've been thinking about, Mex," he remarked in his usual mild drawl, "to have forgot all about a Christmas present I got to give. I'm going to ride over tomorrow night and shoot Madison Lane in his own house. He got my girl—Rosita would have had me if he hadn't cut into the game. I wonder why I happened to overlook it up to now?"

"Ah, shucks, Kid," said Mexican, "don't talk foolishness. You know you can't get within a mile of Mad Lane's house tomorrow night. I see old man Allen day before yesterday, and he says Mad is going to have Christmas doings at his house. You remember how you shot up the festivities when Mad was married, and about the threats you made? Don't you suppose Mad Lane'll kind of keep his eye open for a certain

Mr. Kid? You plumb make me tired, Kid, with such remarks."

"I'm going," repeated the Frio Kid, without heat, "to go to Madison Lane's Christmas doings, and kill him. I ought to have done it a long time ago. Why, Mex, just two weeks ago I dreamed me and Rosita was married instead of her and him; and we was living in a house, and I could see her smiling at me, and—oh! Mex, he got her; and I'll get him—yes, sir, on Christmas Eve he got her, and then's when I'll get him."

"There's other ways of committing suicide," advised Mexican. "Why don't you go and surrender to the sheriff?"

"I'll get him," said the Kid.

Christmas Eve fell as balmy as April. Perhaps there was a hint of faraway frostiness in the air, but it tingled like seltzer, perfumed faintly with late prairie blossoms and the mesquite grass.

When night came the five or six rooms of the ranch house were brightly lit. In one room was a Christmas tree, for the Lanes had a boy of three, and a dozen or more guests were expected from the nearer ranches.

At nightfall Madison Lane called aside Jim Belcher and three other cowboys employed on his ranch.

"Now, boys," said Lane, "keep your eyes open. Walk around the house and watch the road well. All of you know the 'Frio Kid,' as they call him now, and if you see him, open fire on him without asking any questions. I'm not afraid of his coming around, but Rosita is. She's been afraid he'd come in on us every Christmas since we were married."

"I think there is a spot of good somewhere in everybody."

The guests had arrived in buckboards and on horseback, and were making themselves comfortable inside.

The evening went along pleasantly. The guests enjoyed and praised Rosita's excellent supper, and afterwards the men scattered in groups about the rooms or on the broad "gallery," smoking and chatting.

The Christmas tree, of course, delighted the youngsters, and above all were they pleased when Santa Claus himself in magnificent white beard and furs appeared and began to distribute the toys.

"It's my papa," announced Billy Sampson, aged six. "I've seen him wear 'em before."

Berkly, a sheepman, old friend of Lane, stopped Rosita as she was passing by him on the gallery, where he was sitting smoking.

"Well, Mrs. Lane," said he, "I suppose by this Christmas you've gotten over being afraid of that fellow McRoy, haven't you? Madison and I have talked about it, you know."

"Very nearly," said Rosita, smiling, "but I am still nervous sometimes. I shall never forget that awful time when he came so near to killing us."

"He's the most coldhearted villain in the world," said Berkly. "The citizens all along the border ought to turn out and hunt him down like a wolf."

"He has committed awful crimes," said Rosita, "but—I—don't—know. I think there is a spot of good somewhere in everybody. He was not always bad—that I know."

Rosita turned into the hallway between the rooms. Santa Claus, in muffling whiskers and furs, was just coming
through.

"I heard what you said through the window, Mrs. Lane," he
said. "I was just going down in my pocket for a Christmas
present for your husband. But I've left one for you, instead. It's
in the room to your right."

"Oh, thank you, kind Santa Claus," said Rosita, brightly.

Rosita went into the room, while Santa Claus stepped into
the cooler air of the yard.

She found no one in the room but Madison.

"Where is my present that Santa said he left for me in
here?" she asked.

"Haven't seen anything in the way of a present," said her
husband, laughing, "unless he could have meant me."

The next day Gabriel Radd, a foreman of the XO Ranch,
dropped into the post office at Loma Alta.

"Well, the Frio Kid's got his dose of lead at last," he
remarked to the postmaster.

"That so? How'd it happen?"

"One of old Sanchez's Mexican sheepherders did it!
Think of it! The Frio Kid killed by a sheepherder! He saw
him riding along past his camp about twelve o'clock last

night, and was so skeered that he up with a Winchester and let him have it. Funniest part of it was that the Kid was dressed all up with white Angora-skin whiskers and a regular Santy Claus rig-out from head to foot. Think of the Frio Kid playing Santy!"

SPRINGTIME
À LA CARTE

~⌒⌒~

I t was a day in March.

Never, never begin a story this way when you write one. No opening could possibly be worse. It is unimaginative, flat dry, and likely to consist of mere wind. But in this instance it is allowable. For the following paragraph, which should have inaugurated the narrative, is too wildly extravagant and preposterous to be flaunted in the face of the reader without preparation.

Sarah was crying over her bill of fare.

Think of a New York girl shedding tears on the menu card!

To account for this you will be allowed to guess that the lobsters were all out, or that she had sworn ice cream off during Lent, or that she had ordered onions. And then, all these theories being wrong, you will please let the story proceed.

The gentleman who announced that the world was an oyster which he with his sword would open made a larger hit than he deserved. It is not difficult to open an oyster with a sword. But did you ever notice anyone try to open the terrestrial bivalve with a typewriter? Like to wait for a dozen raw opened that way?

Sarah had managed to pry apart the shells with her unhandy weapon far enough to nibble a wee bit at the cold and clammy world within. She knew no more shorthand than if she had been a graduate in stenography just let slip upon the world by a business college. So, not being able to stenog, she could not enter that bright galaxy of office talent. She was a freelance typewriter and canvassed for odd jobs of copying.

The most brilliant and crowning feat of Sarah's battle with the world was the deal she made with Schulenberg's Home Restaurant. The restaurant was next door to the old red brick in which she hall-roomed. One evening after dining at Schulenberg's forty-cent, five-course *table d'hôte* Sarah took away with her the bill of fare. It was written in an almost unreadable script neither English nor German, and so arranged that if you were not careful you began with a toothpick and rice pudding and ended with soup and the day of the week.

The next day Sarah showed Schulenberg a neat card on which the menu was beautifully typewritten with the viands temptingly marshaled under their right and proper heads from "hors d'oeuvre" to "not responsible for overcoats and umbrellas."

Schulenberg became a naturalized citizen on the spot. Before Sarah left him she had him willingly committed to an agreement. She was to furnish typewritten bills of fare for the twenty-one tables in the restaurant—a new bill for each day's dinner, and new ones for breakfast and lunch as often as changes occurred in the food or as neatness required.

In return for this Schulenberg was to send three meals per diem to Sarah's hall room by a waiter—an obsequious one if possible—and furnish her each afternoon with a pencil draft of what Fate had in store for Schulenberg's customers on the morrow.

Mutual satisfaction resulted from the agreement. Schulenberg's patrons now knew what the food they ate was called, even if its nature sometimes puzzled them. And Sarah had food during a cold, dull winter, which was the main thing with her.

And then the almanac lied, and said that spring had come. Spring comes when it comes. The frozen snows of January still lay like adamant in the crosstown streets. The hand organs still played "In the Good Old Summertime," with their December vivacity and expression. Men began to make thirty-day notes to buy Easter dresses. Janitors shut off steam. And when these things happen one may know that the city is still in the clutches of winter.

One afternoon Sarah shivered in her elegant hall bedroom; "house heated; scrupulously clean; conveniences; seen to be appreciated." She had no work to do except Schulenberg's menu cards. Sarah sat in her squeaky willow rocker, and looked out the window. The calendar on the wall kept crying to her: "Springtime is here, Sarah—springtime is here, I tell you. Look at me, Sarah, my figures show it. You've got a neat figure yourself, Sarah—a—nice springtime figure—why do you look out the window so sadly?"

Sarah's room was at the back of the house. Looking out the window she could see the windowless rear brick wall of the box factory on the next street. But the wall was clearest crystal; and Sarah was looking down a grassy lane shaded with cherry trees and elms and bordered with raspberry bushes and Cherokee roses.

Spring's real harbingers are too subtle for the eye and ear. Some must have the flowering crocus, the wood-starring dogwood, the voice of bluebird—even so gross a reminder as the farewell handshake of the retiring buckwheat and oyster before they can welcome the Lady in Green to their dull bosoms. But to old earth's choicest kind there come straight, sweet messages from his newest bride, telling them they shall be no stepchildren unless they choose to be.

On the previous summer Sarah had gone into the country and loved a farmer.

(In writing your story never hark back thus. It is bad art, and cripples interest. Let it march, march.)

Sarah stayed two weeks at Sunnybrook Farm. There she learned to love old Farmer Franklin's son Walter. Farmers have been loved and wedded and turned out to grass in less time. But young Walter Franklin was a modern agriculturist. He had a telephone in his cow house, and he could figure up exactly what effect next year's Canada wheat crop would have on potatoes planted in the dark of the moon.

It was in this shaded and raspberried lane that Walter had wooed and won her. And together they had sat and woven a crown of dandelions for her hair. He had immoderately praised the effect of the yellow blossoms against her brown tresses; and she had left the chaplet there, and walked back to the house swinging her straw sailor in her hands.

They were to marry in the spring—at the very first signs of spring, Walter said. And Sarah came back to the city to pound her typewriter.

A knock at the door dispelled Sarah's visions of that happy day. A waiter had brought the rough pencil draft of the Home Restaurant's next day fare in old Schulenberg's angular hand.

Sarah sat down to her typewriter and slipped a card between the rollers. She was a nimble worker. Generally in an hour and a half the twenty-one menu cards were written and ready.

Today there were more changes on the bill of fare than usual. The soups were lighter; pork was eliminated from the entrées, figuring only with Russian turnips among the roasts. The gracious spirit of spring pervaded the entire menu. Lamb, that lately capered on the greening hillsides, was becoming exploited with the sauce that commemorated its gambols. The song of the oyster, though not silenced, was *dimuendo con amore*. The frying pan seemed to be held, inactive, behind the beneficent bars of the broiler. The pie list swelled; the richer puddings had vanished; the sausage, with his drapery wrapped about him, barely lingered in a pleasant thanatopsis with the buckwheats and the sweet but doomed maple.

Sarah's fingers danced like midgets above a summer stream. Down through the courses she worked, giving each item its position according to its length with an accurate eye.

Just above the desserts came the list of vegetables. Carrots and peas, asparagus on toast, the perennial tomatoes and corn and succotash, lima beans, cabbage—and then—

Sarah was crying over her bill of fare. Tears from the depths of some divine despair rose in her heart and gathered to her eyes. Down went her head on the little typewriter stand; and the keyboard rattled a dry accompaniment to her moist sobs.

For she had received no letter from Walter in two weeks, and the next item on the bill of fare was dandelions—dandelions with some kind of egg—but bother the egg!—dandelions, with whose golden blooms Walter had crowned her his queen of love and future bride—dandelions, the harbingers of spring, her sorrow's crown of sorrow—reminder of her happiest days.

Madam, I dare you to smile until you suffer this test. Let the Marechal Niel roses that Percy brought you on the night you gave him your heart be served as a salad with French dressing before your eyes at a Schulenberg *table d'hôte*. Had Juliet so seen her love tokens dishonored the sooner would she have sought the lethean herbs of the good apothecary.

But what witch is Spring! Into the great cold city of stone and iron a message had to be sent. There was none to convey it but the little hardy courier of the fields with his rough green coat and modest air. He is a true soldier of fortune, this *dent-de-lion*—this lion's tooth, as the French chefs call him. Flowered, he will assist at lovemaking, wreathed in my lady's nut-brown hair; young and callow and unblossomed, he goes into the boiling pot and delivers the word of his sovereign mistress.

By and by Sarah forced back her tears. The cards must be written. But, still in a faint, golden glow from her dandelion dream, she fingered the typewriter keys absently for a little while, with her mind and heart in the meadow lane with her young farmer. But soon she came swiftly back to the rockbound lanes of Manhattan, and the typewriter began to rattle and jump like a strikebreaker's motor car.

Still in a faint, golden glow from her dandelion dream.

At six o'clock the waiter brought her dinner and carried away the typewritten bill of fare. When Sarah ate she set aside, with a sigh, the dish of dandelions with its crowning ovarious accompaniment. As this dark mass had been transformed from a bright and love-endorsed flower to be an ignominious vegetable, so had her summer hopes wilted and perished. Love may, as Shakespeare said, feed on itself: but Sarah could not bring herself to eat the dandelions that had graced, as ornaments, the first spiritual banquet of her heart's true affection.

At seven-thirty the couple in the next room began to quarrel; the man in the room above sought for A on his flute; the gas went a little lower; three coal wagons started to unload— the only sound of which the phonograph is jealous; cats on the back fences slowly retreated toward Mukden. By these signs Sarah knew that it was time for her to read. She got out *The Cloister and the Hearth,* the best nonselling book of the month, settled her feet on her trunk, and began to wander with Gerard.

The front doorbell rang. The landlady answered it. Sarah left Gerard and Denys treed by a bear and listened. Oh, yes; you would, just as she did!

And then a strong voice was heard in the hall below, and Sarah jumped for her door, leaving the book on the floor and the first round easily the bear's.

You have guessed it. She reached the top of the stairs just as her farmer came up, three at a jump, and reaped and garnered her, with nothing left for the gleaners.

"Why haven't you written—oh, why?" cried Sarah.

"New York is a pretty large town," said Walter Franklin. "I came in a week ago to your old address. I found that you went away on a Thursday. That consoled some; it eliminated the possible Friday bad luck. But it didn't prevent my hunting for you with police and otherwise ever since!"

"I wrote!" said Sarah, vehemently.

"Never got it!"

"Then how did you find me?"

The young farmer smiled a springtime smile.

"I dropped into the Home Restaurant next door this evening," said he. "I don't care who knows it; I like a dish of some kind of green at this time of the year. I ran my eye down that nice typewritten bill of fare looking for something in that line. When I got below cabbage I turned my chair over and hollered for the proprietor. He told me where you lived."

"I remember," sighed Sarah, happily. "That was dandelions below cabbage."

"I'd know that cranky capital W 'way above the line that your typewriter makes anywhere in the world," said Franklin.

"Why, there's no W in dandelions," said Sarah in surprise.

The young man drew the bill of fare from his pocket and pointed to a line.

Sarah recognized the first card she had typewritten that afternoon. There was still the rayed splotch in the upper right-hand corner where a tear had fallen. But over the spot where one should have read the name of the meadow plant, the clinging memory of their golden blossoms had allowed her fingers to strike strange keys.

Between the red cabbage and the stuffed green peppers was the item:

"DEAREST WALTER, WITH HARD-BOILED EGG."

ROADS OF DESTINY

I go to seek on many roads
What is to be.
True heart and strong, with love to light—
Will they not bear me in the fight
To order, shun or wield or mold
My Destiny?
UNPUBLISHED POEMS OF DAVID MIGNOT

The song was over. The words were David's; the air, one of the countryside. The company about the inn table applauded heartily, for the young poet paid for the wine. Only the notary, M. Papineau, shook his head a little at the lines, for he was a man of books, and he had not drunk with the rest.

David went out into the village street, where the night air drove the wine vapor from his head. And then he remembered that he and Yvonne had quarreled that day, and that he had resolved to leave his home that night to seek fame and honor in the great world outside.

"When my poems are on every man's tongue," he told himself, in a fine exhilaration, "she will, perhaps, think of the hard words she spoke this day."

Except the roisterers in the tavern, the village folk were abed. David crept softly into his room in the shed of his father's cottage and made a bundle of his small store of clothing. With this upon a staff, he set his face outward upon the road that ran from Vernoy.

He passed his father's herd of sheep huddled in their nightly pen—the sheep he herded daily, leaving them to scatter while he wrote verses on scraps of paper. He saw a light yet shining in Yvonne's window, and a weakness shook his purpose of a sudden. Perhaps that light meant that she rued, sleepless, her anger, and that morning might— But, no! His decision was made. Vernoy was no place for him. Not one soul there could share his thoughts. Out along that road lay his fate and his future.

Three leagues across the dim, moonlit champaign ran the road, straight as a plowman's furrow. It was believed in the village that the road ran to Paris, at least; and this name the poet whispered often to himself as he walked. Never so far from Vernoy had David traveled before.

THE LEFT BRANCH *Three leagues, then, the road ran, and turned into a puzzle. It joined with another and a larger road at right angles. David stood, uncertain, for a while, and then took the road to the left.*

✧

Upon this more important highway were, imprinted in the dust, wheel tracks left by the recent passage of some vehicle. Some half an hour later these traces were verified by the sight of a ponderous carriage mired in a little brook at the bottom of a steep hill. The driver and postilions were shouting and tugging at the horses' bridles. On the road at one side stood a huge black-clothed man and a slender lady wrapped in a long, light cloak.

David saw the lack of skill in the efforts of the servants. He quietly assumed control of the work. He directed the outriders to cease their clamor at the horses and to exercise their strength upon the wheels. The driver alone urged the animals with his familiar voice; David himself heaved a powerful shoulder at the rear of the carriage, and with one harmonious tug the great vehicle rolled up on solid ground. The outriders climbed to their places.

David stood for a moment upon one foot. The huge gentleman waved a hand. "You will enter the carriage," he said, in a voice large, like himself, but smoothed by art and habit. Obedience belonged in the path of such a voice. Brief as was the young poet's hesitation, it was cut shorter still by a renewal of the command. David's foot went to the step. In the darkness he perceived dimly the form of the lady upon the rear seat. He was about to seat himself opposite, when the voice again swayed him to its will. "You will sit at the lady's side."

The gentleman swung his great weight to the forward seat. The carriage proceeded up the hill. The lady was shrunk, silent, into her corner. David could not estimate whether she was old or young, but a delicate, mild perfume from her clothes stirred his poet's fancy to the belief that there was loveliness beneath the mystery. Here was an adventure such as he had often imagined. But as yet he held no key to it, for no word was spoken while he sat with his impenetrable companions.

In an hour's time David perceived through the window that the vehicle traversed the street of some town. Then it stopped in front of a closed and darkened house, and a postilion alighted to hammer impatiently upon the door. A latticed window above flew wide and a nightcapped head popped out.

"Who are ye that disturb honest folk at this time of night? My house is closed. 'Tis too late for profitable travelers to be abroad. Cease knocking at my door, and be off."

"Open!" spluttered the postilion, loudly. "Open for Monseigneur the Marquis de Beaupertuys."

"Ah!" cried the voice above. "Ten thousand pardons, my lord. I did not know—the hour is so late—at once shall the door be opened, and the house placed at my lord's disposal."

Inside was heard the clink of chair and bar, and the door was flung open. Shivering with chill and apprehension, the landlord of the Silver Flagon stood, half-clad, candle in hand, upon the threshold.

David followed the marquis out of the carriage. "Assist the

lady," he was ordered. The poet obeyed. He felt her small hand tremble as he guided her descent. "Into the house," was the next command.

The room was the long dining hall of the tavern. A great oak table ran down its length. The huge gentleman seated himself in a chair at the nearer end. The lady sank into another against the wall, with an air of great weariness. David stood, considering how best he might now take his leave and continue upon his way.

"My lord," said the landlord, bowing to the floor, "h-had I ex-expected this honor, entertainment would have been ready. T-t-there is wine and cold fowl and m-m-maybe—"

"Candles," said the marquis, spreading the fingers of one plump white hand in a gesture he had.

"Y-yes, my lord." He fetched half a dozen candles, lighted them, and set them upon the table.

"If monsieur would, perhaps, deign to taste a certain Burgundy—there is a cask—"

"Candles," said monsieur, spreading his fingers.

"Assuredly—quickly—I fly, my lord."

A dozen more lighted candles shone in the hall. The great bulk of the marquis overflowed his chair. He was dressed in fine black from head to foot save for the snowy ruffles at his wrist and throat. Even the hilt and scabbard of his sword were black. His expression was one of sneering pride. The ends of an upturned mustache reached nearly to his mocking eyes.

The lady sat motionless, and now David perceived that she was young, and possessed a pathetic and appealing beauty. He was startled from the contemplation of her forlorn loveliness by the booming voice of the marquis.

"What is your name and pursuit?"

"David Mignot. I am a poet."

The mustache of the marquis curled nearer to his eyes.

"How do you live?"

"I am also a shepherd; I guarded my father's flock," David answered, with his head high, but a flush upon his cheek.

"Then listen, master shepherd and poet, to the fortune you have blundered upon tonight. This lady is my niece, Mademoiselle Lucie de Varennes. She is of noble descent and is possessed of ten thousand francs a year in her own right. As to her charms, you have but to observe for yourself. If the inventory pleases your shepherd's heart, she becomes your wife at a word. Do not interrupt me. Tonight I conveyed her to the château of the Comte de Villemaur, to whom her hand had been promised. Guests were present; the priest was waiting; her marriage to one eligible in rank and fortune was ready to be accomplished. At the altar this demoiselle, so meek and dutiful, turned upon me like a leopardess, charged me with cruelty and crimes, and broke, before the gaping priest, the troth I had plighted for her. I swore there and then, by ten thousand devils, that she should marry the first man we met after leaving the château, be he prince, charcoal burner, or thief. You, shepherd, are the first. Mademoiselle must be wed this night. If not you, then another. You have ten minutes in which to make your decision. Do not vex me with words or questions. Ten minutes, shepherd; and they are speeding."

The marquis drummed loudly with his white fingers upon the table. He sank into a veiled attitude of waiting. It was as if some great house had shut its doors and windows against approach. David would have spoken, but the huge man's bearing stopped his tongue. Instead, he stood by the lady's chair and bowed.

"Mademoiselle," he said, and he marveled to find his words flowing easily before so much elegance and beauty. "You have heard me say I was a shepherd. I have also had the fancy, at times, that I am a poet. If it be the test of a poet to adore and cherish the beautiful, that fancy is now strengthened. Can I serve you in any way, mademoiselle?"

The young woman looked up at him with eyes dry and mournful. His frank, glowing face, made serious by the gravity of the adventure, his strong, straight figure and the liquid sympathy in his blue eyes, perhaps, also, her imminent need of long-denied help and kindness, thawed her to sudden tears.

"Monsieur," she said, in low tones, "you look to be true and kind. He is my uncle, the brother of my father, and my only relative. He loved my mother, and he hates me because I am like her. He has made my life one long terror. I am afraid of his very looks, and never before dared to disobey him. But tonight he would have married me to a man three times my age. You will forgive me for bringing this vexation upon you, monsieur. You will, of course, decline this mad act he tries to force upon you. But let me thank you for your generous words, at least. I have had none spoken to me in so long."

There was now something more than generosity in the poet's eyes. Poet he must have been, for Yvonne was forgotten; this fine, new loveliness held him with its freshness and grace. The subtle perfume from her filled him with strange emotions. His tender look fell warmly upon her. She leaned to it, thirstily.

"Ten minutes," said David, "is given me in which to do what I would devote years to achieve. I will not say I pity you, mademoiselle; it would not be true—I love you. I cannot ask love from you yet, but let me rescue you from this cruel man, and, in time, love may come. I think I have a future, I will not always be a shepherd. For the present I will cherish you with all my heart and make your life less sad. Will you trust your fate to me, mademoiselle?"

"Ah, you would sacrifice yourself from pity!"

"From love. The time is almost up, mademoiselle."

"You will regret it, and despise me."

"I will live only to make you happy, and myself worthy of you."

Her fine small hand crept into his from beneath her cloak.

"I will trust you," she breathed, "with my life. And—and

love—may not be so far off as you think. Tell him. Once away from the power of his eyes I may forget."

David went and stood before the marquis. The black figure stirred, and the mocking eyes glanced at the great hall clock.

"Two minutes to spare. A shepherd requires eight minutes to decide whether he will accept a bride of beauty and income! Speak up, shepherd, do you consent to become mademoiselle's husband?"

"Mademoiselle," said David, standing proudly, "has done me the honor to yield to my request that she become my wife."

"Well said!" said the marquis. "You have yet the making of a courtier in you, master shepherd. Mademoiselle could have drawn a worse prize, after all. And now to be done with the affair as quick as the Church and the devil will allow!"

He struck the table soundly with his sword hilt. The landlord came, knee-shaking, bringing more candles in the hope of anticipating the great lord's whims. "Fetch a priest," said the marquis, "a priest; do you understand? In ten minutes have a priest here, or—"

The landlord dropped his candles and flew.

The priest came heavy-eyed and ruffled. He made David Mignot and Lucie de Varennes man and wife, pocketed a gold piece that the marquis tossed him, and shuffled out again into the night.

"Wine," ordered the marquis, spreading his ominous fingers at the host.

"Fill glasses," he said, when it was brought. He stood up at the head of the table in the candlelight, a black mountain of venom and conceit, with something like the memory of an old love turned to poison in his eye, as it fell upon his niece.

"Monsieur Mignot," he said, raising his wineglass, "drink after I say this to you. You have taken to be your wife one who will make your life a foul and wretched thing. The blood in her is an inheritance running black lies and red ruin. She will bring you shame and anxiety. The devil that descended to her is there in her eyes and skin and mouth that stoop even to beguile a peasant. There is your promise, monsieur poet, for a happy life. Drink your wine. At last, mademoiselle, I am rid of you."

The marquis drank. A little grievous cry, as if from a sudden wound, came from the girl's lips. David, with his glass in his hand, stepped forward three paces and faced the marquis. There was little of a shepherd in his bearing.

"Just now," he said calmly, "you did me the honor to call me 'monsieur.' May I hope, therefore, that my marriage to mademoiselle has placed me somewhat nearer to you in—let us say, reflected rank, and has given me the right to stand more as an equal to monseigneur in a certain little piece of business I have in my mind?"

"You may hope, shepherd," sneered the marquis.

"Then," said David, dashing his glass of wine into the contemptuous eyes that mocked him, "perhaps you will condescend to fight me."

The fury of the great lord outbroke in one sudden curse like a blast from a horn. He tore his sword from its black sheath; he called to the hovering landlord: "A sword there, for this lout!" He turned to the lady, with a laugh that chilled her heart, and said: "You put much labor upon me, madame. It seems I must find you a husband and make you a widow in the same night."

"I know not swordplay," said David. He flushed to make the confession before his lady.

"'I know not swordplay,'" mimicked the marquis. "Shall we fight like peasants with oaken cudgels? *Hola!* François, my pistols!"

A postilion brought two shining great pistols ornamented with carven silver from the carriage holsters. The marquis tossed one upon the table near David's hand. "To the other end of the table," he cried; "even a shepherd may pull a trigger. Few of them attain the honor to die by the weapon of a de Beaupertuys."

The shepherd and the marquis faced each other from the ends of the long table. The landlord, in an ague of terror, clutched the air and stammered: "M-M-Monseigneur, for the love of Christ! Not in my house! Do not spill blood—it will ruin my custom—" The look of the marquis, threatening him, paralyzed his tongue.

"Coward," cried the lord of Beaupertuys, "cease chattering your teeth long enough to give the word for us, if you can."

Mine host's knees smote the floor. He was without a vocabulary. Even sounds were beyond him. Still, by gestures he seemed to beseech peace in the name of his house and custom.

"I will give the word," said the lady, in a clear voice. She went up to David and kissed him sweetly. Her eyes were sparkling bright, and color had come to her cheek. She stood against the wall, and the two men leveled their pistols for her count.

"*Un—deux—trois!*"

The two reports came so nearly together that the candles flickered but once. The marquis stood, smiling, the fingers of his left hand resting, outspread, upon the end of the table. David remained erect, and turned his head very slowly, searching for his wife with his eyes. Then, as a garment falls from where it is hung, he sank, crumpled, upon the floor.

With a little cry of terror and despair, the widowed maid ran and stooped above him. She found his wound, and then looked up with her old look of pale melancholy. "Through his heart," she whispered. "Oh, his heart!"

"Come," boomed the great voice of the marquis, "out with you to the carriage! Daybreak shall not find you on my hands. Wed you shall be again, and to a living husband, this night. The next we come upon, my lady, highwayman or peasant. If the road yields no other, then the churl that opens my gates. Out with you to the carriage!"

The marquis, implacable and huge, the lady wrapped again in the mystery of her cloak, the postilion bearing the weapons—all moved out to the waiting carriage. The sound of

its ponderous wheels rolling away echoed through the slumber-
ing village. In the hall of the Silver Flagon the distracted landlord wrung his hands above the slain poet's body, while the
flames of the four and twenty candles danced and flickered on
the table.

THE RIGHT BRANCH *Three leagues, then, the road ran, and turned
into a puzzle. It joined with another and a larger road at right
angles. David stood, uncertain, for a while, and then took the road
to the right.*

Whither it led he knew not, but he was resolved to leave
Vernoy far behind that night. He traveled a league and then
passed a large château which showed testimony of recent
entertainment. Lights shone from every window; from the
great stone gateway ran a tracery of wheel tracks drawn in the
dust by the vehicles of the guests.

Three leagues farther and David was weary. He rested and
slept for a while on a bed of pine boughs at the roadside. Then
up and on again along the unknown way.

Thus for five days he traveled the great road, sleeping upon
Nature's balsamic beds or in peasants' ricks, eating of their
black, hospitable bread, drinking from streams or the willing
cup of the goatherd.

At length he crossed a great bridge and set his foot within
the smiling city that has crushed or crowned more poets than

all the rest of the world. His breath came quickly as Paris sang to him in a little undertone her vital chant of greeting—the hum of voice and foot and wheel.

High up under the eaves of an old house in the Rue Conti, David paid for lodging, and set himself, in a wooden chair, to his poems. The street, once sheltering citizens of import and consequence, was now given over to those who ever follow in the wake of decline.

The houses were tall and still possessed of a ruined dignity, but many of them were empty save for dust and the spider. By night there was the clash of steel and the cries of brawlers straying restlessly from inn to inn. Where once gentility abode was now but a rancid and rude incontinence. But here David found housing commensurate to his scant purse. Daylight and candlelight found him at pen and paper.

One afternoon he was returning from a foraging trip to the lower world, with bread and curds and a bottle of thin wine. Halfway up his dark stairway he met—or rather came upon, for she rested on the stair—a young woman of a beauty that should balk even the justice of a poet's imagination. A loose, dark cloak, flung open, showed a rich gown beneath. Her eyes changed swiftly with every little shade of thought. Within one moment they would be round and artless like a child's, and long and cozening like a gypsy's. One hand raised her gown, undraping a nude shoe, high-heeled, with its ribbons dangling, untied. So heavenly she was, so unfitted to stoop, so qualified to charm and command! Perhaps she had seen David coming, and had waited for his help there.

Ah, would monsieur pardon that she occupied the stairway, but the shoe! The naughty shoe! Alas! It would not remain tied. Ah! If monsieur *would* be so gracious!

The poet's fingers trembled as he tied the contrary ribbons. Then he would have fled from the danger of her presence, but the eyes grew long and cozening, like a gypsy's, and held him. He leaned against the balustrade, clutching his bottle of sour wine.

"You have been so good," she said, smiling. "Does monsieur, perhaps, live in the house?"

"Yes, madame. I—I think so, madame."

"Perhaps in the third story, then?"

"No, madame; higher up."

The lady fluttered her fingers with the least possible gesture of impatience.

"Pardon. Certainly I am not discreet in asking. Monsieur will forgive me? It is surely not becoming that I should inquire where he lodges."

"Madame, do not say so. I live in the—"

"No, no, no; do not tell me. Now I see that I erred. But I cannot lose the interest I feel in this house and all that is in it. Once it was my home. Often I come here but to dream of those happy days again. Will you let that be my excuse?"

"Let me tell you, then, for you need no excuse," stammered

the poet. "I live in the top floor—the small room where the stairs turn."

"In the front room?" asked the lady, turning her head side-wise.

"The rear, madame."

The lady sighed, as if with relief.

"I will detain you no longer, then, monsieur," she said, employing the round and artless eye. "Take good care of my house. Alas! Only the memories of it are mine now. Adieu, and accept my thanks for your courtesy."

She was gone, leaving but a smile and a trace of sweet per-fume. David climbed the stairs as one in slumber. But he awoke from it, and the smile and the perfume lingered with him and never afterward did either seem quite to leave him. This lady of whom he knew nothing drove him to lyrics of eyes, chansons of swiftly conceived love, odes to curling hair, and sonnets to slippers on slender feet.

Poet he must have been, for Yvonne was forgotten; this fine, new loveliness held him with its freshness and grace. The subtle perfume about her filled him with strange emotions.

On a certain night three persons were gathered about a table in a room on the third floor of the same house. Three chairs and the table and a lighted candle upon it was all the furni-ture. One of the persons was a huge man, dressed in black. His expression was one of sneering pride. The ends of his upturned mustache reached nearly to his mocking eyes. Another was a lady, young and beautiful, with eyes that could be round and artless, like a child's, or long and cozening, like a gypsy's, but were now keen and ambitious, like any other conspirator's. The third was a man of action, a combatant, a bold and impatient executive, breathing fire and steel. He was addressed by the others as Captain Desrolles.

This man struck the table with his fist, and said, with controlled violence:

"Tonight. Tonight as he goes to midnight mass. I am tired of the plotting that gets nowhere. I am sick of signals and ciphers and secret meetings and such *baragouin*. Let us be honest traitors. If France is to be rid of him, let us kill in the open, and not hunt with snares and traps. Tonight, I say. I back my words. My hand will do the deed. Tonight, as he goes to mass."

The lady turned upon him a cordial look. Woman, however wedded to plots, must ever thus bow to rash courage. The big man stroked his upturned mustache.

"Dear captain," he said, in a great voice, softened by habit, "this time I agree with you. Nothing is to be gained by waiting. Enough of the palace guards belong to us to make the endeavor a safe one."

"Tonight," repeated Captain Desrolles, again striking the table. "You have heard me, marquis; my hand will do the deed."

"But now," said the huge man, softly, "comes a question.

Word must be sent to our partisans in the palace, and a signal agreed upon. Our staunchest men must accompany the royal carriage. At this hour what messenger can penetrate so far as the south doorway? Ribout is stationed there; once a message is placed in his hands, all will go well."

"I will send the message," said the lady.

"You, countess?" said the marquis, raising his eyebrows. "Your devotion is great, we know, but—"

"Listen!" exclaimed the lady, rising and resting her hands upon the table. "In a garret of this house lives a youth from the provinces as guileless and tender as the lambs he tended there. I have met him twice or thrice upon the stairs. I questioned him, fearing that he might dwell too near the room in which we are accustomed to meet. He is mine, if I will. He writes poems in his garret, and I think he dreams of me. He will do what I say. He shall take the message to the palace."

The marquis rose from his chair and bowed. "You did not permit me to finish my sentence, countess," he said. "I would have said: 'Your devotion is great, but your wit and charm are infinitely greater.'"

While the conspirators were thus engaged, David was polishing some lines addressed to his *amorette d'escalier*. He heard a timorous knock at his door, and opened it, with a great throb, to behold her there, panting as one in straits, with eyes wide open and artless, like a child's.

"Monsieur," she breathed, "I come to you in distress. I

believe you to be good and true, and I know of no other help. How I flew through the streets among the swaggering men! Monsieur, my mother is dying. My uncle is a captain of guards in the palace of the king. Someone must fly to bring him. May I hope—"

"Mademoiselle," interrupted David, his eyes shining with the desire to do her service, "your hopes shall be my wings. Tell me how I may reach him."

The lady thrust a sealed paper into his hand.

"Go to the south gate—the south gate, mind—and say to the guards there, 'The falcon has left his nest.' They will pass you, and you will go to the south entrance to the palace. Repeat the words, and give this letter to the man who will reply 'Let him strike when he will.' This is the password, monsieur, entrusted to me by my uncle, for now when the country is disturbed and men plot against the king's life, no one without it can gain entrance to the palace grounds after nightfall. If you will, monsieur, take him this letter so that my mother may see him before she closes her eyes."

"Give it me," said David, eagerly. "But shall I let you return home through the streets alone so late? I—"

"No, no—fly. Each moment is like a precious jewel. Sometime," said the lady, with eyes long and cozening, like a gypsy's, "I will try to thank you for your goodness."

The poet thrust the letter into his breast, and bounded down the stairway. The lady, when he was gone, returned to the room below.

The eloquent eyebrows of the marquis interrogated her.

"He is gone," she said, "as fleet and stupid as one of his own sheep, to deliver it."

The table shook again from the batter of Captain Desrolles's fist.

"Sacred name!" he cried. "I have left my pistols behind! I can trust no others."

"Take this," said the marquis, drawing from beneath his cloak a shining, great weapon, ornamented with carven silver. "There are none truer. But guard it closely, for it bears my arms and crest, and already I am suspected. Me, I must put many leagues between myself and Paris this night. Tomorrow must find me in my château. After you, dear countess."

The marquis puffed out the candle. The lady, well-cloaked, and the two gentlemen softly descended the stairway and flowed into the crowd that roamed along the narrow pavements of the Rue Conti.

David sped. At the south gate of the king's residence a halberd was laid to his breast, but he turned its point with the words: "The falcon has left his nest."

"Pass, brother," said the guard, "and go quickly."

On the south steps of the palace they moved to seize him, but again the *mot de passe* charmed the watchers. One among them stepped forward and began: "Let him strike—" But a flurry among the guards told of a surprise. A man of keen look and soldierly stride suddenly pressed through them and seized the letter which David held in his hand.

"Come with me," he said, and led him inside the great hall. Then he tore open the letter and read it. He beckoned to a man uniformed as an officer of musketeers, who was passing. "Captain Tetreau, you will have the guards at the south entrance and the south gate arrested and confined. Place men known to be loyal in their places." To David he said: "Come with me."

He conducted him through a corridor and an anteroom into a spacious chamber, where a melancholy man, somberly dressed, sat brooding in a great leather-covered chair. To that man he said:

"Sire, I have told you that the palace is as full of traitors and spies as a sewer is of rats. You have thought, sire, that it was my fancy. This man penetrated to your very door by their connivance. He bore a letter which I have intercepted. I have brought him here that your majesty may no longer think my zeal excessive."

"I will question him," said the king, stirring in his chair. He looked at David with heavy eyes dulled by an opaque film. The poet bent his knee.

"From where do you come?" asked the king.

"From the village of Vernoy, in the province of Eure-et-Loir, sire."

"What do you follow in Paris?"

"I—I would be a poet, sire."

"What did you in Vernoy?"

"I minded my father's flock of sheep."

The king stirred again, and the film lifted from his eyes.

"Ah! In the fields?"

"Yes, sire."

"You lived in the fields; you went out in the cool of the morning and lay among the hedges in the grass. The flock distributed itself upon the hillside; you drank of the living stream; you ate your sweet brown bread in the shade; and you listened, doubtless, to blackbirds piping in the grove. Is not that so, shepherd?"

"It is, sire," answered David, with a sigh; "and to the bees at the flowers, and, maybe, to the grape gatherers singing on the hill."

"Yes, yes," said the king, impatiently; "maybe to them; but surely to the blackbirds. They whistled often, in the grove, did they not?"

"Nowhere, sire, so sweetly as in Eure-et-Loir. I have endeavored to express their song in some verses that I have written."

"Can you repeat those verses?" asked the king eagerly. "A long time ago I listened to the blackbirds. It would be something better than a kingdom if one could rightly construe their song. And at night you drove the sheep to the fold and then sat, in peace and tranquility, to your pleasant bread. Can you repeat those verses, shepherd?"

"They run this way, sire," said David, with respectful ardor:

"Lazy shepherd, see you lambkins
Skip, ecstatic, on the mead;
See the firs dance in the breezes,
Hear Pan blowing at his reed.

"Hear us calling from the treetops,
See us swoop upon your flock;
Yield us wool to make our nests warm
In the branches of the—"

"If you please, your majesty," interrupted a harsh voice, "I will ask a question or two of this rhymester. There is little time to spare. I crave pardon, sire, if my anxiety for your safety offends."

"The loyalty," said the king, "of the Duke d'Aumale is too well proven to give offense." He sank into his chair, and the film came again over his eyes.

"First," said the duke, "I will read you the letter he brought:

"Tonight is the anniversary of the dauphin's death. If he goes,
as is his custom, to midnight mass to pray for the soul of his son,
the falcon will strike, at the corner of the Rue Esplanade. If this
be his intention, set a red light in the upper room at the southwest
corner of the palace, that the falcon may take heed.

"Peasant," said the duke, sternly, "you have heard these words. Who gave you this message to bring?"

"My lord duke," said David, sincerely, "I will tell you. A lady gave it me. She said her mother was ill, and that this writing would fetch her uncle to her bedside. I do not know the meaning of the letter, but I will swear that she is beautiful and good."

"Describe the woman," commanded the duke, "and how you came to be her dupe."

"Describe her!" said David with a tender smile. "You would command words to perform miracles. Well, she is made of sunshine and deep shade. She is slender, like the alders, and moves with their grace. Her eyes change while you gaze into them; now round, and then half shut as the sun peeps between two clouds. When she comes, heaven is all about her; when she leaves, there is chaos and a scent of hawthorn blossoms. She came to me in the Rue Conti, number twenty-nine."

"It is the house," said the duke, turning to the king, "that we have been watching. Thanks to the poet's tongue, we have a picture of the infamous Countess Quebedaux."

"Sire and my lord duke," said David, earnestly, "I hope my poor words have done no injustice. I have looked into that lady's eyes. I will stake my life that she is an angel, letter or no letter."

The duke looked at him steadily. "I will put you to the proof," he said, slowly. "Dressed as the king, you shall, yourself, attend mass in his carriage at midnight. Do you accept the test?"

David smiled. "I have looked into her eyes," he said. "I had my proof there. Take yours how you will."

Half an hour before twelve the Duke d'Aumale, with his own hands, set a red lamp in a southwest window of the palace. At ten minutes to the hour, David, leaning on his arm, dressed as the king, from top to toe, with his head bowed in his cloak, walked slowly from the royal apartments to the waiting carriage. The duke assisted him inside and closed the door. The carriage whirled away along its route to the cathedral.

On the *qui vive* in a house at the corner of the Rue Esplanade was Captain Tetreau with twenty men, ready to pounce upon the conspirators when they should appear.

But it seemed that, for some reason, the plotters had slightly altered their plans. When the royal carriage had reached the Rue Christopher, one square nearer than the Rue Esplanade, forth from it burst Captain Desrolles, with his band of would-be regicides, and assailed the equipage. The guards upon the carriage, though surprised at the premature attack, descended and fought valiantly. The noise of conflict attracted the force of Captain Tetreau, and they came pelting down the street to the rescue. But, in the meantime, the desperate Desrolles had torn open the door of the king's carriage, thrust his weapon against the body of the dark figure inside, and fired.

Now, with loyal reinforcements at hand, the street rang with cries and the rasp of steel, but the frightened horses had dashed away. Upon the cushions lay the dead body of the poor

mock king and poet, slain by a ball from the pistol of
Monseigneur, the Marquis of Beaupertuys.

THE MAIN ROAD *Three leagues, then, the road ran, and turned into
a puzzle. It joined with another and a larger road at right angles.
David stood, uncertain, for a while, and then sat himself to rest
upon its side.*

Whither those roads led he knew not. Either way there
seemed to lie a great world full of chance and peril. And then,
sitting there, his eye fell upon a bright star, one that he and
Yvonne had named for theirs. That set him thinking of
Yvonne, and he wondered if he had not been too hasty. Why
should he leave her and his home because a few hot words had
come between them? Was love so brittle a thing that jealousy,
the very proof of it, could break it? Mornings always brought a
cure for the little heartaches of evening. There was yet time
for him to return home without anyone in the sweetly sleeping
village of Vernoy being the wiser. His heart was Yvonne's;
there where he had lived always he could write his poems and
find his happiness.

David rose, and shook off his unrest and the wild mood
that had tempted him. He set his face steadfastly back along
the road he had come. By the time he had retraveled the road
to Vernoy, his desire to rove was gone. He passed the sheep-
fold, and the sheep scurried, with a drumming flutter, at his

late footsteps, warming his heart by the homely sound. He crept without noise into his little room and lay there, thankful that his feet had escaped the distress of new roads that night.

How well he knew woman's heart! The next evening Yvonne was at the well in the road where the young congregated in order that the *curé* might have business. The corner of her eye was engaged in a search for David, albeit her set mouth seemed unrelenting. He saw the look; braved the mouth, drew from it a recantation and, later, a kiss as they walked homeward together.

Three months afterward they were married. David's father was shrewd and prosperous. He gave them a wedding that was heard of three leagues away. Both the young people were favorites in the village. There was a procession in the streets, a dance on the green; they had the marionettes and a tumbler out from Dreux to delight the guests.

Then a year, and David's father died. The sheep and the cottage descended to him. He already had the seemliest wife in the village. Yvonne's milk pails and her brass kettles were bright—*ouf!* They blinded you in the sun when you passed that way. But you must keep your eyes upon her yard, for flower beds were so neat and gay they restored to you your sight. And you might hear her sing, aye, as far as the double chestnut tree above Père Gruneau's blacksmith forge.

But a day came when David drew out paper from a long-shut drawer, and began to bite the end of a pencil. Spring had come again and touched his heart. Poet he must have been, for now Yvonne was well-nigh forgotten. This fine new loveliness of earth held him with its witchery and grace. The perfume from her woods and meadows stirred him strangely. Daily had he gone forth with his flock, and brought it safe at night. But now he stretched himself under the hedge and pieced words together on his bits of paper. The sheep strayed, and the wolves, perceiving that difficult poems make easy mutton, ventured from the woods and stole his lambs.

David's stock of poems grew larger and his flock smaller. Yvonne's nose and temper waxed sharp and her talk blunt. Her pans and kettles grew dull, but her eyes had caught their flash. She pointed out to the poet that his neglect was reducing the flock and bringing woe upon the household. David hired a boy to guard the sheep, locked himself in the little room in the top of the cottage, and wrote more poems. The boy, being a poet by nature, but not furnished with an outlet in the way of writing, spent his time in slumber. The wolves lost no time in discovering that poetry and sleep are practically the same; so the flock steadily grew smaller. Yvonne's ill temper increased at an equal rate. Sometimes she would stand in the yard and rail at David through his high window. Then you could hear her as far as the double chestnut tree above Père Gruneau's blacksmith forge.

M. Papineau, the kind, wise, meddling old notary, saw this, as he saw everything at which his nose pointed. He went to

David, fortified himself with a great pinch of snuff, and said:

"Friend Mignot, I affixed the seal upon the marriage certifi-cate of your father. It would distress me to be obliged to attest a paper signifying the bankruptcy of his son. But that is what you are coming to. I speak as an old friend. Now, listen to what I have to say. You have your heart set, I perceive, upon poetry. At Dreux, I have a friend, one Monsieur Bril—Georges Bril. He lives in a little cleared space in a houseful of books. He is a learned man; he visits Paris each year; he himself has written books. He will tell you when the catacombs were made, how they found out the names of the stars, and why the plover has a long bill. The meaning and the form of poetry is to him as intelligent as the baa of a sheep is to you. I will give you a let-ter to him, and you shall take him your poems and let him read them. Then you will know if you shall write more, or give your attention to your wife and business."

"Write the letter," said David. "I am sorry you did not speak of this sooner."

At sunrise the next morning he was on the road to Dreux with the precious roll of poems under his arm. At noon he wiped the dust from his feet at the door of Monsieur Bril. That learned man broke the seal of M. Papineau's letter, and sucked up its contents through his gleaming spectacles as the sun draws water. He took David inside to his study and sat him down upon a little island beat upon by a sea of books.

Monsieur Bril had a conscience. He flinched not even at a

David locked himself in the little room and wrote more poems.

mass of manuscript the thickness of a finger length and rolled to an incorrigible curve. He broke the back of the roll against his knee and began to read. He slighted nothing; he bored into the lump as a worm into a nut, seeking for a kernel.

Meanwhile, David sat, marooned, trembling in the spray of so much literature. It roared in his ears. He held no chart or compass for voyaging in that sea. Half the world, he thought, must be writing books.

Monsieur Bril bored to the last page of the poems. Then he took off his spectacles and wiped them with his handkerchief.

"My old friend, Papineau, is well?" he asked.

"In the best of health," said David.

"How many sheep have you, Monsieur Mignot?"

"Three hundred and nine, when I counted them yesterday. The flock has had ill fortune. To that number it has decreased from eight hundred and fifty."

"You have a wife and a home, and lived in comfort. The sheep brought you plenty. You went into the fields with them and lived in the keen air and ate the sweet bread of contentment. You had but to be vigilant and recline there upon nature's breast, listening to the whistle of the blackbirds in the grove. Am I right thus far?"

"It was so," said David.

"I have read all your verses," continued Monsieur Bril, his eyes wandering about his sea of books as if he conned the horizon for a sail. "Look yonder, through that window, Monsieur Mignot; tell me what you see in that tree."

"I see a crow," said David, looking.

"There is a bird," said Monsieur Bril, "that shall assist me where I am disposed to shirk a duty. You know that bird, Monsieur Mignot; he is the philosopher of the air. He is happy through submission to his lot. None so merry or full-crawed as he with his whimsical eye and rollicking step. The fields yield him what he desires. He never grieves that his plumage is not gay, like the oriole's. And you have heard, Monsieur Mignot, the notes that nature has given him? Is the nightingale any happier, do you think?"

David rose to his feet. The crow cawed harshly from his tree.

"I thank you, Monsieur Bril," he said, slowly. "There was not, then, one nightingale note among all those croaks?"

"I could not have missed it," said Monsieur Bril, with a sigh. "I read every word. Live your poetry, man; do not try to write it any more."

"I thank you," said David, again. "And now I will be going back to my sheep."

"If you would dine with me," said the man of books, "and overlook the smart of it, I will give you reasons at length."

"No," said the poet, "I must be back in the fields cawing at my sheep."

Back along the road to Vernoy he trudged with his poems under his arm. When he reached his village he turned into the shop of one Zeigler, a Jew out of Armenia, who sold anything that came to his hand.

"Friend," said David, "wolves from the forest harass my sheep on the hills. I must purchase firearms to protect them. What have you?"

"A bad day, this, for me, friend Mignot," said Zeigler, spreading his hands, "for I perceive that I must sell you a weapon that will not fetch a tenth of its value. Only last week I bought from a peddler a wagon full of goods that he procured at a sale by a *commissionaire* of the crown. The sale was of the château and belongings of a great lord—I know not his title—who has been banished for conspiracy against the king. There are some choice firearms in the lot. This pistol—oh, a weapon fit for a prince!—it shall be only forty francs to you, friend Mignot—if I lost ten by the sale. But perhaps an arquebus—"

"This will do," said David, throwing the money on the counter. "Is it charged?"

"I will charge it," said Zeigler. "And, for ten francs more, add a store of powder and ball."

David laid his pistol under his coat and walked to his cottage. Yvonne was not there. Of late she had taken to gadding much among the neighbors. But a fire was glowing in the kitchen stove. David opened the door of it and thrust his poems in upon the coals. As they blazed up they made a singing, harsh sound in the flue.

"The song of the crow!" said the poet.

He went up to his attic room and closed the door. So quiet was the village that a score of people heard the roar of the great pistol. They flocked thither, and up the stairs where the smoke, issuing, drew their notice.

The men laid the body of the poet upon his bed, awkwardly arranging it to conceal the torn plumage of the poor black crow. The women chattered in a luxury of zealous pity. Some of them ran to tell Yvonne.

M. Papineau, whose nose had brought him there among the first, picked up the weapon and ran his eye over its silver mountings with a mingled air of connoisseurship and grief.

"The arms," he explained, aside, to the *curé*, "and crest of Monseigneur, the Marquis de Beaupertuys."

THE GIFT

OF

THE MAGI

One dollar and eighty-seven cents. That was all. And sixty cents of it was in pennies. Pennies saved one and two at a time by bulldozing the grocer and the vegetable man and the butcher until one's cheeks burned with the silent imputation of parsimony that such close dealing implied. Three times Della counted it. One dollar and eighty-seven cents. And the next day would be Christmas.

There was clearly nothing to do but flop down on the shabby little couch and howl. So Della did it. Which instigates the moral reflection that life is made of sobs, sniffles, and smiles, with sniffles predominating.

While the mistress of the home is gradually subsiding from the first stage to the second, take a look at the home. A furnished flat at eight dollars per week. It did not exactly beggar description, but it certainly had that word on the lookout for the mendicancy squad.

In the vestibule below was a letter box into which no letter would go, and an electric button from which no mortal finger could coax a ring. Also appertaining thereunto was a card bearing the name "Mr. James Dillingham Young."

The "Dillingham" had been flung to the breeze during a former period of prosperity when its possessor was being paid thirty dollars per week. Now, when the income was shrunk to twenty dollars, the letters of "Dillingham" looked blurred, as though they were thinking seriously of contracting to a modest and unassuming D. But whenever Mr. James Dillingham Young came home and reached his flat above ·he was called "Jim" and greatly hugged by Mrs. James Dillingham Young, already introduced to you as Della. Which is all very good.

Della finished her cry and attended to her cheeks with the powder rag. She stood by the window and looked out dully at a gray cat walking a gray fence in a gray backyard. Tomorrow would be Christmas Day, and she had only one dollar and eighty-seven cents with which to buy Jim a present. She had been saving every penny she could for months, with this result. Twenty dollars a week doesn't go far. Expenses had been greater than she had calculated. They always are. Only one dollar and eighty-seven cents to buy a present for Jim. Her Jim. Many a happy hour she had spent planning for something nice for him. Something fine and rare and sterling—something just a little bit near to being worthy of the honor of being owned by Jim.

There was a pier glass between the windows of the room. Perhaps you have seen a pier glass in an eight-dollar flat. A very thin and very agile person may, by observing his reflection in a rapid sequence of longitudinal strips, obtain a fairly accurate conception of his looks. Della, being slender, had mastered the art.

Suddenly she whirled from the window and stood before the glass. Her eyes were shining brilliantly, but her face had lost its color within twenty seconds. Rapidly she pulled down her hair and let it fall to its full length.

Now, there were two possessions of the James Dillingham Youngs in which they both took a mighty pride. One was Jim's gold watch, which had been his father's and his grandfather's. The other was Della's hair. Had the Queen of Sheba lived in the flat across the air shaft, Della would have let her hair hang out the window someday to dry just to depreciate Her Majesty's jewels and gifts. Had King Solomon been the janitor, with all his treasures piled up in the basement, Jim would have pulled out his watch every time he passed, just to see him pluck at his beard from envy.

So now Della's beautiful hair fell about her, rippling and

shining like a cascade of brown waters. It reached below her knee and made itself almost a garment for her. And then she did it up again nervously and quickly. Once she faltered for a minute and stood still while a tear or two splashed on the worn red carpet.

On went her old brown jacket; on went her old brown hat. With a whirl of skirts and with the brilliant sparkle still in her eyes, she fluttered out the door and down the stairs to the street.

Where she stopped the sign read: "Mme. Sofronie. Hair Goods of All Kinds." One flight up Della ran, and collected herself, panting. Madame, large, too white, chilly, hardly looked the "Sofronie."

"Will you buy my hair?" asked Della.

"I buy hair," said Madame. "Take yer hat off and let's have a sight at the looks of it."

Down rippled the brown cascade.

"Twenty dollars," said Madame, lifting the mass with a practiced hand.

"Give it to me quick," said Della.

Oh, and the next two hours tripped by on rosy wings. Forget the hashed metaphor. She was ransacking the stores for Jim's present.

She found it at last. It surely had been made for Jim and no one else. There was no other like it in any of the stores, and she had turned all of them inside out. It was a platinum fob

Rippling and shining like a cascade of brown waters.

chain simple and chaste in design, properly proclaiming its value by substance alone and not by meretricious ornamentation—as all good things should do. It was even worthy of The Watch. As soon as she saw it she knew that it must be Jim's. It was like him. Quietness and value—the description applied to both. Twenty-one dollars they took from her for it, and she hurried home with the eighty-seven cents. With that chain on his watch Jim might be properly anxious about the time in any company. Grand as the watch was, he sometimes looked at it on the sly on account of the old leather strap that he used in place of a chain.

When Della reached home her intoxication gave way a little to prudence and reason. She got out her curling irons and lighted the gas and went to work repairing the ravages made by generosity added to love. Which is always a tremendous task, dear friends—a mammoth task.

Within forty minutes her head was covered with tiny, close-lying curls that made her look wonderfully like a truant schoolboy. She looked at her reflection in the mirror long, carefully, and critically.

"If Jim doesn't kill me," she said to herself, "before he takes a second look at me, he'll say I look like a Coney Island chorus girl. But what could I do—oh! What could I do with a dollar and eighty-seven cents?"

At seven o'clock the coffee was made and the frying pan was on the back of the stove, hot and ready to cook the chops.

Jim was never late. Della doubled the fob chain in her hand and sat on the corner of the table near the door that he always entered. Then she heard his step on the stair away down on the first flight, and she turned white for just a moment. She had a habit of saying little silent prayers about the simplest everyday things, and now she whispered: "Please God, make him think I am still pretty."

The door opened and Jim stepped in and closed it. He looked thin and very serious. Poor fellow, he was only twenty-two—and to be burdened with a family! He needed a new overcoat and he was without gloves.

Jim stopped inside the door, as immovable as a setter at the scent of quail. His eyes were fixed upon Della, and there was an expression in them that she could not read, and it terrified her. It was not anger, nor surprise, nor disapproval, nor horror, nor any of the sentiments that she had been prepared for. He simply stared at her fixedly with that peculiar expression on his face.

Della wriggled off the table and went for him.

"Jim, darling," she cried, "don't look at me that way. I had my hair cut off and sold it because I couldn't have lived through Christmas without giving you a present. It'll grow out again—you won't mind, will you? I just had to do it. My hair grows awfully fast. Merry Christmas, Jim, and let's be happy. You don't know what a nice—what a beautiful, nice gift I've got for you."

"You've cut off your hair?" asked Jim, laboriously, as if he had not arrived at that patent fact yet even after the hardest mental labor.

"Cut it off and sold it," said Della. "Don't you like me just as well, anyhow? I'm me without my hair, ain't I?"

Jim looked about the room curiously.

"You say your hair is gone?" he said, with an air almost of idiocy.

"You needn't look for it," said Della. "It's sold, I tell you—sold and gone, too. It's Christmas Eve, boy. Be good to me, for it went for you. Maybe the hairs on my head were numbered," she went on with a sudden serious sweetness, "but nobody could ever count my love for you. Shall I put the chops on, Jim?"

Out of his trance Jim seemed quickly to wake. He enfolded his Della. For ten seconds let us regard with discreet scrutiny some inconsequential object in the other direction. Eight dollars a week or a million a year—what is the difference? A mathematician or a wit would give you the wrong answer. The magi brought valuable gifts, but that was not among them. This dark assertion will be illuminated later on.

Jim drew a package from his overcoat pocket and threw it upon the table.

"Don't make any mistake, Dell," he said, "about me. I don't think there's anything in the way of a haircut or a shave or a shampoo that could make me like my girl any less. But if you'll unwrap that package you may see why you had me going awhile at first."

White fingers and nimble tore at the string and paper. And then an ecstatic scream of joy; and then—alas!—a quick feminine charge to hysterical tears and wails, necessitating the immediate employment of all the comforting powers of the lord of the flat.

For there lay The Combs—the set of combs, side and back, that Della had worshiped for long in a Broadway window. Beautiful combs, pure tortoiseshell, with jeweled rims—just the shade to wear in the beautiful vanished hair. They were expensive combs, she knew, and her heart had simply craved and yearned over them without the least hope of possession. And now, they were hers, but the tresses that should have adorned the coveted adornments were gone.

But she hugged them to her bosom, and at length she was able to look up with dim eyes and a smile and say: "My hair grows so fast, Jim!"

And then Della leaped up like a little singed cat and cried, "Oh, oh!"

Jim had not yet seen his beautiful present. She held it out to him eagerly upon her open palm. The dull precious metal seemed to flash with a reflection of her bright and ardent spirit.

"Isn't it a dandy, Jim? I hunted all over town to find it. You'll have to look at the time a hundred times a day now.

Give me your watch. I want to see how it looks on it."

Instead of obeying, Jim tumbled down on the couch and put his hands under the back of his head and smiled.

"Dell," said he, "let's put our Christmas presents away and keep 'em awhile. They're too nice to use just at present. I sold the watch to get the money to buy your combs. And now suppose you put the chops on."

The magi, as you know, were wise men—wonderfully wise men—who brought gifts to the Babe in the manger. They invented the art of giving Christmas presents. Being wise, their gifts were no doubt wise ones, possibly bearing the privilege of exchange in case of duplication. And here I have lamely related to you the uneventful chronicle of two foolish children in a flat who most unwisely sacrificed for each other the greatest treasures of their house. But in a last word to the wise of these days let it be said that of all who give gifts these two were the wisest. Of all who give and receive gifts, such as they are wisest. Everywhere they are wisest. They are the magi.

AFTERWORD

❧

William Sydney Porter—better known to readers
everywhere by his pseudonym, O. Henry—was born
in Greensboro, North Carolina, in 1862. Following
the death of his mother when he was only three, Porter was
raised by an indifferent father. The boy's sole source of reading
material and encouragement for his early writing efforts came
from an aunt who ran a private school.

At age twenty, Porter traveled to Texas to work on a sheep
farm. The young man gained acceptance from the cowboys, as
well as literary material. Years later, the cowboys' many anec-

dotes served as the basis for such unforgettable stories as "The Pimienta Pancakes."

In 1887, Porter married a young Texan woman. While working as a draftsman at the General Land Office, he gained a reputation as a cartoonist and started his own weekly comic magazine, *The Rolling Stone*. The collapse of the magazine after only a few issues left him deeply in debt, and he took a job as a teller at the First National Bank in Austin. But when approximately one thousand dollars in discrepancies turned up in his accounts, Porter was discharged. To this day no one knows for sure if Porter was innocent or not, but when a warrant was issued for his arrest the following year, he fled to Mexico rather than face prosecution.

Three years later, in 1898, Porter returned to Texas to be with his seriously ill wife. He was arrested on a charge of embezzlement, convicted, and sentenced to five years in prison. But rather than break his spirit, prison seemed to inspire Porter. Drawing on the many people he had met in his travels and the colorful characters he now met behind bars, he began to write and submit stories to small magazines under the pen name O. Henry. His stories first began to appear in 1899 and 1900.

Paroled for good behavior after serving three years of his sentence, Porter, now widowed, moved to Pittsburgh, where he began to write at a furious pace, submitting story after story to numerous New York editors. Offered a guaranteed income by the editor of *Ainslee's* magazine if he would move to New York, Porter settled there in 1902 and soon became fascinated by its many and varied citizens. Turning out one wonderful story after the next, he established himself over the next eight years as one of the most well-known and appreciated writers of short stories in literary history.

For this new collection, we have selected some of O. Henry's very best stories, from his hilarious tales of outrageous cowboys and clever con men to yarns with surprise twists about happy vagrants and foolish "men of means" to heart-warming tales of tender—yet ironic—love. Michael Dooling's striking paintings capture the gentle drama and high-spirited mirth of these timeless stories.

Filled with wry humor, gentle humanity, and his signature offbeat surprise endings, the stories of O. Henry are today universally loved and admired. Drawn from real people he met and infused with his own humorous yet compassionate view of the human condition, they remain some of the most poignant and amusing tales in American literature.

—*Peter Glassman*

BOOKS OF WONDER CLASSICS

DELUXE GIFT EDITIONS OF TIMELESS STORIES,
LAVISHLY ILLUSTRATED WITH FULL-COLOR PLATES AND BLACK-AND-WHITE DRAWINGS

THE ARABIAN NIGHTS
retold by Brian Alderson
illustrated by Michael Foreman

THE SECRET GARDEN
by Frances Hodgson Burnett
illustrated by S. Saelig Gallagher

ALICE'S ADVENTURES IN WONDERLAND
by Lewis Carroll
illustrated by John Tenniel

THROUGH THE LOOKING-GLASS
by Lewis Carroll
illustrated by John Tenniel

THE TROJAN WAR AND
THE ADVENTURES OF ODYSSEUS
by Padraic Colum
illustrated by Barry Moser

A CHRISTMAS CAROL
by Charles Dickens
illustrated by Carter Goodrich

OLIVER TWIST
by Charles Dickens
illustrated by Don Freeman

THE ADVENTURES OF SHERLOCK HOLMES
by Sir Arthur Conan Doyle
illustrated by Barry Moser

THE WHITE COMPANY
by Sir Arthur Conan Doyle
illustrated by N. C. Wyeth

THE THREE MUSKETEERS
by Alexandre Dumas
illustrated by Tom Kidd

THE MAGICAL LAND OF NOOM
written and illustrated by Johnny Gruelle

THE GIFT OF THE MAGI
by O. Henry
illustrated by Michael Dooling

THE LEGEND OF SLEEPY HOLLOW
by Washington Irving
illustrated by Arthur Rackham

RIP VAN WINKLE
by Washington Irving
illustrated by N. C. Wyeth

THE WATER-BABIES
by Charles Kingsley
illustrated by Jessie Willcox Smith

THE JUNGLE BOOK
by Rudyard Kipling
illustrated by Jerry Pinkney

JUST SO STORIES
by Rudyard Kipling
illustrated by Barry Moser

THE RAINBOW FAIRY BOOK
by Andrew Lang
illustrated by Michael Hague

THE STORY OF DOCTOR DOLITTLE
by Hugh Lofting
illustrated by Michael Hague

AT THE BACK OF THE NORTH WIND
by George MacDonald
illustrated by Jessie Willcox Smith

THE PRINCESS AND THE GOBLIN
by George MacDonald
illustrated by Jessie Willcox Smith

GREAT GHOST STORIES
selected and illustrated by Barry Moser

THE ENCHANTED CASTLE
by E. Nesbit
illustrated by Paul O. Zelinsky

FIVE CHILDREN AND IT
by E. Nesbit
illustrated by Paul O. Zelinsky

TALES OF EDGAR ALLAN POE
by Edgar Allan Poe
illustrated by Barry Moser

BLACK BEAUTY
by Anna Sewell
illustrated by Lucy Kemp-Welch

HEIDI
by Johanna Spyri
illustrated by Jessie Willcox Smith

A CHILD'S GARDEN OF VERSES
by Robert Louis Stevenson
illustrated by Diane Goode

DRACULA
by Bram Stoker
illustrated by Barry Moser

THE ADVENTURES OF HUCKLEBERRY FINN
by Mark Twain
illustrated by Steven Kellogg

THE ADVENTURES OF TOM SAWYER
by Mark Twain
illustrated by Barry Moser

A CONNECTICUT YANKEE
IN KING ARTHUR'S COURT
by Mark Twain
illustrated by Trina Schart Hyman

AROUND THE WORLD IN EIGHTY DAYS
by Jules Verne
illustrated by Barry Moser

20,000 LEAGUES UNDER THE SEA
by Jules Verne
illustrated by Leo and Diane Dillon

REBECCA OF SUNNYBROOK FARM
by Kate Douglas Wiggin
illustrated by Helen Mason Grose

THE HAPPY PRINCE AND OTHER STORIES
by Oscar Wilde
illustrated by Charles Robinson

OZ TITLES IN THE
BOOKS OF WONDER SERIES

THE WONDERFUL WIZARD OF OZ
by L. Frank Baum
with 24 full-color plates and over 130 two-color illustrations
by W. W. Denslow

THE MARVELOUS LAND OF OZ
by L. Frank Baum
with 16 full-color plates and over 125 black-and-white illustrations
by John R. Neill

OZMA OF OZ
by L. Frank Baum
with 42 full-color and 21 two-color illustrations
by John R. Neill

DOROTHY AND THE WIZARD IN OZ
by L. Frank Baum
with 16 full-color plates and 50 black-and-white illustrations
by John R. Neill

THE ROAD TO OZ
by L. Frank Baum
with 126 black-and-white illustrations on multicolored paper
by John R. Neill

THE EMERALD CITY OF OZ
by L. Frank Baum
with 16 full-color plates and 90 black-and-white illustrations
by John R. Neill

THE PATCHWORK GIRL OF OZ
by L. Frank Baum
with 51 full-color and 80 black-and-white illustrations
by John R. Neill

TIK-TOK OF OZ
by L. Frank Baum
with 12 full-color plates and 78 black-and-white illustrations
by John R. Neill

THE SCARECROW OF OZ
by L. Frank Baum
with 12 full-color plates and 104 black-and-white illustrations
by John R. Neill

RINKITINK IN OZ
by L. Frank Baum
with 12 full-color plates and 97 black-and-white illustrations
by John R. Neill

THE LOST PRINCESS OF OZ
by L. Frank Baum
with 12 full-color plates and 98 black-and-white illustrations
by John R. Neill

THE TIN WOODMAN OF OZ
by L. Frank Baum
with 12 full-color plates and 92 black-and-white illustrations
by John R. Neill

THE MAGIC OF OZ
by L. Frank Baum
with 12 full-color plates and 104 black-and-white illustrations
by John R. Neill

GLINDA OF OZ
by L. Frank Baum
with 12 full-color plates and and 91 black-and-white illustrations

LITTLE WIZARD STORIES OF OZ
by L. Frank Baum
with 45 full-color illustrations
by John R. Neill

DOROTHY OF OZ
by Roger S. Baum
with full-color frontispiece and 50 black-and-white illustrations
by Elizabeth Miles

OZ: THE HUNDREDTH ANNIVERSARY CELEBRATION
edited by Peter Glassman
with art and text in appreciation of OZ
by thirty favorite artists and writers

If you enjoy the Oz books and want to know more about Oz, you may be interested in
The Royal Club of Oz. Devoted to America's favorite fairyland, it is a club for everyone
who loves the Oz books. For free information, please send a first-class stamp to:

THE ROYAL CLUB OF OZ
P.O. Box 714
New York, New York 10011
or call toll free: (800) 207-6968